A KILT FOR CHRISTMAS
THE ENCHANTED HIGHLANDS
BOOK THREE

TRICIA O'MALLEY

LOVEWRITE PUBLISHING

A Kilt for Christmas
AN ENCHANTED HIGHLANDS SERIES STAND-ALONE NOVEL

Copyright © 2023 by Lovewrite Publishing
All Rights Reserved

Editors: Marion Archer; David Burness

All rights reserved. No part of this book may be reproduced in any form by any means without express permission of the author. This includes reprints, excerpts, photocopying, recording, or any future means of reproducing text.

If you would like to do any of the above, please seek permission first by contacting the author at: info@triciaomalley.com

"I don't want a lot for Christmas, there's just one thing I need." – Mariah Carey

GLOSSARY OF SCOTTISH WORDS/SLANG

- Away and shite – On you go, that's enough.
- Bit o' banter – Scots love to tease each other; banter is highly cherished
- Bloody – a word used to add emphasis; expletive
- Bonnie – pretty
- Brekkie – breakfast
- Clarty – dirty
- Coorie – cozy
- He's class – nice, high quality
- Drookit – extremely wet; drenched
- Eejit – idiot
- Gutted – upset, beside myself
- "It's a dreich day" – cold; damp; miserable
- Mate – friend, buddy
- Och – used to express many emotions, typically surprise, regret, or disbelief
- On you go then – be on your way; get on with it
- Shoogly – unsteady; wobbly

- Tetchy – crabby, cranky, moody
- Tea – in Scotland, having tea is often used to refer to the dinnertime meal
- Wee – small, little
- Wheesht (haud your wheesht) – be quiet, hush, shut up

CHAPTER ONE

West

I wasn't exactly sure how I'd managed to convince myself that a winter vacation in Scotland was going to cure my impending burnout, and now, as I faced the wall of icy rain that stood between my rental cottage and the local pub, I questioned my impulsive decision. On average, California saw around two hundred and eighty days of sunshine. Any of which I could have used to disconnect from the all-consuming demands of a tenure-track professorship, budget cuts, and students with dwindling attention spans. Instead, my colleague, Matthew, had convinced me that a trip to Loren Brae to visit his best friend Sophie—and to enjoy the winter book festival—was exactly what I needed.

Books, I liked.

Christmas? I could give or take.

Biting rain and a damp that permeated the marrow of my bones? Yeah, I could leave that. The wind shifted, spraying my glasses with a fine mist of rain, and I sighed as I pulled them off and wiped the lenses with my pocket square. Futile gesture, I supposed, if I planned to trudge to the pub for my supper. The Airbnb description had insisted that the cottage was only a short walk into the village of Loren Brae, but I was just now realizing that my definition of a short walk varied significantly from a Scottish one. Perhaps this was simply a case of "lost in translation," however, by my calculations, I'd have at least a thirty-minute walk into the small village that hugged the banks of Loch Mirren. On a cheerful spring day, which is when the pictures of the online rental listing had likely been taken, I'm sure it was a lovely jaunt. Now, however, I was seriously considering going to sleep without my supper.

The taxi driver who delivered me from the airport had informed me that he lived two villages over and was going home for the night for a birthday party and there would be nobody else on duty. Which meant, I could walk, go to sleep and ignore my hunger pains, or ... my eyes landed on a bicycle tucked under a small lean-to on the side of the cottage. *That's right*. I'd forgotten the cottage came with a bike. Whether I walked or biked, there was no avoiding getting wet. However, with the bike I might be able to get through the worst of it quickly.

Ducking back inside the cottage, I went to find my rain jacket. While the location of the cottage might have been a touch misrepresented, the description of the house itself had been spot on. A quaint one-bedroom with stone walls, wood beams crossing the ceiling, and a rustic stone fireplace —the cottage ranked high on the scale for coziness. I certainly wouldn't be giving the outdoor wood-burning hot tub a spin, despite the enthusiastic reviews left in the guest book, and shivered just thinking about having to run outside in the rain to start a fire.

A serviceable bath and a simple bedroom were tucked off the main room of the cottage, and the kitchen was well outfitted for cooking. Frankly, anything away from my roommates was a joy for me. I'd first started sharing a small house by campus with two other professors when I'd taken my job. Rent was high in California, and at the time, it had made sense. What I hadn't planned for was my two roommates falling in love and having such a tumultuous relationship that I felt like I was a guest star on a reality show. If it wasn't screaming arguments and slamming doors, it was X-rated kisses and unavoidable, over-the-top displays of cringeworthy affection that made me start to wonder if I really *was* being filmed. And not for the kind of film that aired on *Lifetime*. At this point, it was a toss-up whether they were going to ask me to referee a fight or join their couple, and I, for one, wasn't interested in either of those positions. Luckily, I'd finally found a new place to live and by the time I returned home from Scotland, I'd be just weeks away from accepting the keys to my new rental.

In the meantime, an ocean seemed the perfect space between me and my roomies, and just the thought of not having to deal with their problems over dinner tonight was enough motivation to lace up my waterproof hiking boots, add a nubby wool sweater, and zip into my rain jacket. Once outside, I ducked under the overhang and examined the bike. Glancing to the street, slick with icy rain that stopped just short of turning to snow, I eyed the tires of the bike dubiously. In my head, the bike had seemed a better solution than trudging through the downpour. *You're a literature professor from California who is not known for his coordination. Biking in the sleet is probably not in your wheelhouse.* Though it pained me to admit it, my thirst for life won out over the annoyance of wet clothes. Returning to the cottage, I snagged the umbrella tucked in a stand next to the door and resigned myself for a soggy walk into town.

The night was quiet in the way of Mother Nature making herself known during a storm. Though it wasn't quite the stillness of a forest after freshly fallen snow, not much warred with the whistle of wind bustling across the frothy waters of Loch Mirren. I was looking forward to seeing the loch in the daylight tomorrow, but for now I contented myself with admiring how the rain dotted the reflection of the village lights on the water's dark surface. It reminded me of a Matisse painting, with thousands of raindrops combining to create a picturesque reflection of Loren Brae. A gust of wind blasted me, carrying with it a salty spray of water from the loch, and a shiver danced down my back.

It felt like I was being watched.

Turning, I squinted through the rain, but nothing appeared in the shadows behind me. The light from my cabin door stood out like a beacon in the darkness. Or was it a warning? I'd read enough novels to wonder if *I* was the intrepid hero already making mistakes on his journey.

"Listen, West. There's more to Loren Brae than you could ever imagine. Honestly, you'll be fascinated, what with the abundant myths and legends surrounding the village. Some ... still around today."

Matthew's words echoed in my mind as I bent my head to the pavement, pulling the umbrella lower as the rain intensified. Quickening my steps, I virtually ran toward town, the sturdy soles of my boots keeping me safe from falling. I wasn't sure if I was running to get out of the rain, or from the hint of something watching me in the darkness, but by the time I'd arrived at the door of the pub, I was panting with exertion.

And a little bit of excitement.

I felt like a kid who'd worked himself up when having to run down into a dark basement to grab something from the storage for his parents. With an overactive imagination, it was easy to convince myself that monsters lurked in dark corners, and with Matthew's warning dancing in my head, I was half-certain that Loren Brae really *was* haunted.

Pulling open the door to the pub, appropriately named The Tipsy Thistle, conversation boomed around me, and a spicy garlic scent enticed my already growling stomach. Shaking off my umbrella in the front hallway, I placed it in one of the several stands near the door and took off my jacket to hang on a coat rack. I cleaned my glasses with my pocket square, ran a hand through my damp hair, and ducked through the low doorway that led to the main pub.

"Perfect. There's the drookit lad we need."

I raised an eyebrow as the entire pub turned to look at me, and despite my confidence in standing in front of a group of silent people, I glanced over my shoulder to make sure the man behind the bar was indeed addressing me.

"Hello?" I asked, and then unable to stop myself, I added, "Is it me you're looking for?"

A slim woman with a short crop of dark curls snickered at the bar and turned to the bartender.

"That should do it. We've enough now to crack on. Let me just tell Maisie—"

"Tell Maisie what?"

I turned and blinked at a woman who stepped into the pub from one of the many doorways leading from the main room. Upon closer inspection, the pub itself seemed to be a hodgepodge collection of rooms and snugs pieced together to create a cozy space. A fire roared in a large fireplace along one thick stone wall, and warm lights made the wood of the circular bar gleam a honey gold. But it wasn't the bar that caught my attention, oh no. It was this woman who stared at me, a cranky expression on her stunning face.

She reminded me of the flame that danced in the fire. Energy seemed to crackle around her, her blue eyes were sharp, and she tossed her mane of dark curls over a shoulder. Even though she didn't step forward, it was as though I wanted to draw closer to her, some sort of magnetic force pulling me in, and she turned an assessing look upon me.

"We've found the fourth for our team." The bartender nodded at me.

"What do you know about trivia?" the prickly goddess asked, interrogating me.

"I know that it derives from the word trivial, which was introduced in the English language around the fifteenth century. As for the game, it was popularized by university students in the sixties," I recited precisely, amusement dancing through me as the woman's eyes narrowed even further. I couldn't quite tell if she approved of me, or my answer, but nevertheless, I was intrigued.

The bartender let out a low whistle, as a clamor went up around the pub.

A KILT FOR CHRISTMAS

"We'll take the lad. Go on then, Graham. Switch him out with Jacob then," a man seated at a table by the fire called.

"I saw him first." The bartender patted the bar in front of an open seat. "Come, my new best friend. Join us."

Crossing the room, I took the offered seat, as an argument broke out behind me.

"His name's not on the card. You have to sign up in advance for quiz night."

"It's hardly our fault that Sophie took ill, is it?" the woman sitting next to me argued.

"Sophie?" I piped in, nodding my thanks as the bartender slid me a menu. "Is that Matthew's friend, Sophie? At the castle?"

"Ah, you're Matthew's friend. I hear he'll be joining us for Christmas." The woman with the short curls and warm eyes offered me a hand. "I'm Agnes. You've arrived just in time for our bi-monthly quiz night."

"I suppose you'll do." The other woman, with all the equanimity of an enraged hedgehog, sniffed and took the other seat next to me. "I'm Maisie, cousin to Agnes, and in town to help her with the Christmas Book Festival."

"I'm Weston Smith, but you can call me West." I smiled as the woman raised an eyebrow at me. *Prickly*. I warmed to her suspicious nature.

"And I'm Graham, owner of this lovely establishment, and if it's food you're wanting, I'll be taking your order as the cook will want to play too."

"What? No sexy lean-in?" Agnes rolled her eyes at Graham. "No deepening of your voice? No wink or sexual innuendo? We're in modern times. Shouldn't all customers get the same treatment?"

"Och, the lass has the right of it," Graham readily agreed and to my surprise, he leaned over and rested his arms on the bar, fixing me with a heavy look. Deepening his brogue, he winked at me. "All right then, lad ... how can I whet your appetite?"

"Should I find this hot? I shouldn't find this hot, right?" Agnes demanded.

"Oh, it's hot," Maisie agreed, fanning her face. I couldn't help but grin in Graham's direction.

"Much to my great sadness, I, alas, do not play for your team." I sighed and shook my head, as though despondent, and Graham chuckled.

"Nor I yours, but this snow queen over here likes to skewer me with her icicles, don't you, lass?" Graham leveled a look at Agnes, who wore an expression torn between annoyance and amusement.

"Queen is a title that I'll happily accept if it means you'll bow to me," Agnes said, baring her teeth at Graham.

"Och, I'll happily get on my knees for you, darling, if you'll be allowing it."

"Bloody hell. Even I'm not that desperate."

"You've been a bit tetchy these days, Agnes. Might do you some good," Graham said, as easily as if he was suggesting that Agnes go for a massage, and Agnes bristled next to me.

"I'll take a bowl of the vegetable soup and the mac and cheese," I interjected, before flames could explode from these two. Were they scorned lovers? "And a pint of the Brewdog Stout."

A warm chuckle from Maisie had my skin tingling, awareness rippling through me, and I turned from where Agnes and Graham seemed on the verge of battle. Or foreplay. It was hard to tell, really.

"So, Maisie, cousin to Agnes, where is home if not here?" I asked, noting how her spiky dark lashes highlighted the brilliant blue of her eyes.

"A few villages up the way." Maisie waved a hand in the air, the highlands lilting in her voice, and shifted in her seat to lean closer to me. "Have you ever been to a quiz night before?"

"A few," I admitted, accepting the pint that Graham slid my way.

"Where?" Maisie demanded.

"In California."

"Well, *Cali*, there are rules here." Maisie glowered at me as though California was a lawless land where trivia nights were run with reckless abandon and a survival of the fittest mentality. My overactive imagination could just see Maisie swaggering down an empty street with a pack of trivia cards at her belt and a mean look in her eye.

"Duly noted," I said, tapping a finger to my forehead in a mock salute. I was rewarded with another narrowed look, and I was feeling suddenly and positively cheerful despite the fact that I was sitting in sodden jeans.

"Rules are meant to be followed." Maisie ticked the rules off on her finger as she listed them. "No phones. No asking other teams for help. No using the bathroom unless it is between rounds."

"I'm guessing you like to win?" I asked, amused at the seriousness of her tone.

"She hasn't lost a quiz night in three years." Agnes nudged an elbow companionably into my arm. "It's why the lads were trying to disqualify her for adding you to the team. She isn't allowed to come to every match or nobody else would ever get a chance to win. It chuffs her off, but her winning streak was getting out of hand."

"Clarty bastards," Maisie muttered, and I grinned into my pint.

Already, I could see why Matthew was so taken with Loren Brae. They were honest yet fun. Intense yet solicitous. Ruthless yet benign. No, it would be tough to get lonely here. *So different to my "normal" life.*

CHAPTER TWO

MAISIE

I wasn't sure who this man with the Clark Kent vibe was, but if he dropped the ball at quiz night, then I didn't care if he was Superman himself, he would be dead to me. Already annoyed that Sophie called in sick, almost rendering our team incapable of playing, I needed to get a quick idea of just what I was dealing with here if I wanted to edge out the other teams. I'd heard talk that Hilda and Archie had been training in their down time, and I wasn't about to mess up my winning streak just because we had a new member on our team. Especially an unknown and untested trivia player.

"What's your win percentage?" I asked West, as Hilda walked around the room distributing quiz cards.

"My win ... percentage?" West's green eyes danced behind his glasses, and I deliberately ignored the shiver in my core. I'd always had a thing for men with green eyes. His were a deep olive, with little flecks of gold around the center, and I was momentarily distracted from my mission.

"Yes, or your ratio. Your record. How else should I phrase it?" I tapped a finger on my lip as I thought about how an American would keep score.

"To be clear, you're asking me what my percentage of wins for quiz nights is back in California?" West tilted his head at me, his perfectly modulated voice sounding faintly like a lecture, and heat licked up my cheeks as I realized that I might be sounding a touch ridiculous.

"Never mind then. No time. Let's move on. What's your background? Where are your strengths? Do you focus heavily in any particular area? Take Graham. He's killer for music facts." I pointed to Graham.

"Ah, well, I've a particular love for—"

A bell clanged loudly, cutting him off, and I tamped down my impatience as Hilda enthusiastically rang a brass handbell to get our attention.

"Welcome to quiz night. For those who are new here, we play twice a month. Each game, we pick a different theme and tonight's theme is Scottish Myths and Legends."

A groan echoed around the room, while excitement danced through me. *This* topic was right up my alley. Though I doubted the American would be of much use here, all I had to do was manage him enough to get the correct answer on the paper. Agnes cast me a delighted look, and I grinned back. Between Agnes, her love of books, and my writing, we were sure to dominate.

"That's hardly fair," Jacob griped from across the room. "Agnes owns a damn bookshop."

"Which is open for all to use if you'd spend your money on a book once in a while," Agnes shot back.

"Okay, West. We aren't expecting you to know much about our literary history, but that's just fine. Agnes owns Bonnie Books and is putting on the Christmas Book Festival, so she's well-primed for a quiz of this nature," I explained, the excitement of competition heating through me. I'd always been this way, likely even when I was a wee bairn. Determined to win at any cost, that drive spilled over into all aspects of my life. Well, almost all. A bitter spot churned in my stomach as my thoughts drifted to my greatest failure to date.

"Ah, a formidable ally in our quest then," West said, a smile quirking his lips, transforming his angular face from interesting to mouthwateringly sexy. It was stunning, really, how quickly my mind bounced from my failed achievements to the bedroom with this man, and yet, here we were. The gift of a vivid imagination.

"And Graham, despite his pretty boy good looks, might have picked up some historical facts here and there." Agnes angled her head at Graham. "Not that he ever opens a book."

Graham gave a lazy smile and leaned closer to Agnes, his voice just a hint over a whisper.

"I'll happily open your—"

"Right, then, let's get on with it. Stuart is our appointed quizmaster this evening." Hilda sat down and bent her head to Archie, a pleased look on her face. The couple were the caretakers at MacAlpine Castle, which held its own stunning library steeped in history. They certainly wouldn't go down without a fight.

"First question." Stuart, a stocky, bald man with a ruddy complexion, brandished a notepad. The pub instantly quieted and everyone bent their heads to their teammates. "In the ballad of Tam Lin, how does the young woman, Janet, save Tam Lin from the Queen of Faeries?"

"It's a trick question," I said immediately, bending close, West and Agnes leaning in. "Janet doesn't save him."

"Yes, she does." West turned to level a look at me, and I stilled as a shiver of ... something ... danced across my skin. At this angle, our faces were only inches apart, and once more I was transfixed by the gold flecks in his eyes.

"No, she doesn't," I argued. "The queen keeps changing Tam Lin into animal forms until she gets him."

"False," West said, so succinctly that I drew back, annoyance replacing my interest. "Janet is so determined to save Tam Lin that she holds on to him until the queen gives up. Her determination saves him."

"That's not how—"

"He's right, Maisie," Agnes hissed, interrupting the beginning of my rant. "That's how the ballad goes."

"It certainly does not. Just because someone is determined to do something, doesn't mean it will happen," I insisted. For a moment, I had the strangest inclination to cry, and I turned to gulp my pint of cider. The cool crisp notes of the drink refreshed me, and I shook my head to clear it. *There's no crying at quiz night.* This wasn't about my own issues, it was about winning. I pressed my lips together as Agnes wrote their answer down on the sheet and slid a look at West. To my surprise, he was watching me with an assessing look, and I shifted in my seat. His eyes seemed to see too much, and I didn't like the flash of sympathy I saw in their depths. Why had we let this man join our team again?

"Next question. What did the Faery Queen use to lure the piper away?"

"Will o' the Wisp," I said at the same time as West, and he grinned. Pleasure rippled through me at his approval, followed quickly by annoyance. I didn't need this man's approval for my answers on quiz night. This was *my* turf. And how the heck does he know these?

"Next question. The Orkney and Shetland islands are meant to have formed from what?"

West tilted his head, pressing his lips together as he considered the question, and I paused, caught on the way his eyes went all dreamy and faraway as he thought through an answer.

"It's about the dragon, isn't it?" I asked, leaning in toward Agnes. My arm brushed West's and a zip of awareness caused my skin to heat.

"Ah, yes. The Norse have a similar myth, don't they?" West asked and I turned, my face now only inches from him. "I'd forgotten that one."

"You know the answer?" Damn it, but intellect on a man was deeply attractive, wasn't it?

"Teeth, right?" West smiled at me, dimples winking in his cheeks, and my heart sighed. Nobody had a right to be this handsome.

"Aye," Agnes said, her tone approving as she marked the answer down. "When the boy killed the serpent, its teeth fell out and formed the islands."

"See? Every serpent falls eventually." Graham winked at Agnes.

"Certainly you're not implying I'm the serpent?" Agnes pointed a finger at her chest, her mouth falling open. "It ate seven virgins for breakfast every Saturday at sunrise."

"Och, that's my bad. You're right, much more *my* style." Graham's grin widened when Agnes looked mad enough to spit, and I quickly intervened.

"Wheesht, next question's up."

"What inspired Robert the Bruce during his darkest time to get up and fight another fight?" The pub ignited with hushed voices at that one, and I smiled.

"A spider," I whispered to West, and he looked at me askance.

"Like in Charlotte's Web?"

"What? No. What's Charlotte's Web?" Now I mirrored West's look of confusion.

"You haven't read Charlotte's Web?" West asked in surprise.

"Or seen the movie?" Agnes leaned in.

"Clearly not, or I'd be nodding my head along now, wouldn't I?" I rolled my eyes as Graham slid me another drink with a cheeky wink.

"Och, Maisie. You have to read it. I've got a copy at the shop."

"What does this have to do with Robert the Bruce?" I asked, a touch annoyed that West and Agnes were in on something that I didn't know about.

"A spider befriends a pig and weaves its messages of encouragement into its web. Much like how Robert the Bruce took inspiration from the spider and coined his famous phrase about try, try again." West's words struck a chord in me, and I turned so he wouldn't see the sadness on my face.

I had been trying. For what felt like ages now. And still, I failed. Stupid spiders. What did they know anyway? Shaking the thoughts away, I raised my drink in a *cheers* to the quizmaster.

We worked our way through the first several rounds of questions fairly easily, with Agnes and me at the helm, though West, surprisingly, seemed to have a grasp on Scottish mythology. I quite enjoyed arguing various points with him, as he offered well-reasoned thoughts for whatever answer he championed. Mostly, I just enjoyed hearing him speak, his crisp American accent sounding like he was addressing a lecture hall. It was only as we approached the last round that would end the game that my nerves kicked up. I'd seen the pleased look on Hilda's face across the pub, and I knew we had to nail these questions to clinch the win.

"The final round will focus on the unicorn, which is Scotland's national animal," Stuart said, leaning closer to read the sheet in his hands. "The first question is: In alchemy, what does the symbol of the unicorn represent?"

"Transformation," West said, not even looking up from where he devoured his food with a ruthless efficiency that I admired. "The symbol of the unicorn is associated with the process of purifying metals to achieve a higher status of being."

I gaped at him, surprised that he would know this answer, and my eyes met Agnes's over his shoulders. She shrugged.

"I'll have to give that one to him. It would track with

other representations of the unicorn across various stories, I suppose." Agnes tapped a finger against her lips and leveled her eyes at the ceiling as she thought about it. Graham just shrugged.

"The lad may have the way of it. Can't say I know much about alchemy."

"Trust me," West said, doggedly consuming his meal. What did this man do that he knew so much about mythology? Since I didn't have the answer, which deeply frustrated me, I lifted a shoulder in acquiescence.

"Write it down." I nodded to Agnes.

"The appearance of a unicorn in mythology is similar to *what* in other cultures' myths?"

"The white stag," West said before I could open my mouth, and I tilted my head at him in question.

"How do you know that?" I demanded, intrigued.

"The white stag is famous across many cultures, all with various meanings, but typically considered a sign of good luck or a harbinger of great change."

"Why does it sound like you're reciting from a book?" I leaned closer, despite my annoyance with him for hijacking my game.

"Casualty of the job, I suppose." West smiled at me, making my insides go liquid again, and I huffed out a breath of annoyance as I turned to confer with Agnes.

"It tracks," Agnes agreed.

"Fine, put it down."

Was it egotistical to want to be the one with all the answers? *Maybe.* Was I taking this Quiz Night Queen label too seriously? *Perhaps.* But in the past few years, fraught with deep personal frustrations, quiz night had kind of become my thing. My ray of sunshine among the dark clouds of stagnation and disappointments if you will.

Yes, I realize that I need to get out more.

"Next question. In Scotland, the unicorn is often depicted wearing chains. The meaning for this has changed through the years. What is the current thought of why a unicorn is seen drawn in chains?"

I slapped my hand on the bar, causing West to drop his spoon into his soup, splattering it across his jumper.

"Sorry," I said, breathless as I grabbed a napkin and absentmindedly wiped the stain on his chest as I spoke. "It's meant to represent power. That the Scottish kings were the only ones powerful enough to tame the untamable."

"While technically correct, that isn't the answer." West looked at me calmly as I suddenly realized that I was blatantly stroking his—admittedly—well-muscled chest. Cheeks burning, I crumpled the napkin and dropped it on the bar, the war of battle lighting my blood.

"It absolutely *is* the answer," I hissed, stopping short of jabbing my finger into his chest. I really needed to not be touching this man, *a stranger*, before I embarrassed myself further. "History shows—"

"Correct, *history* shows. He asked about the *modern* interpretation. The school of thought has shifted in modern ages to Scotland's aspiration for independence and its refusal to be subjugated."

My mouth worked, but no sound came out, as I gaped wordlessly at this man. I shouldn't find his deadpan delivery of historical facts sexy, and yet I was torn between climbing on his lap and kissing that infuriating mouth or throwing my hands up in frustration. Maybe it was the word subjugated that had my mind straying to deliciously naughty thoughts. That had to be it.

"Again, I think he's right," Agnes said, a pained expression on her face. "I have read a few articles about artists that have painted with that viewpoint in mind. If it's modern interpretation he's asking for, well, then that's likely the best answer."

"I'm voting with my mate West. He seems to know the right of it." Graham picked up West's empty pint and held it in the air in question. West nodded and Graham grabbed a fresh glass.

"Seriously? But I … my track record …" I trailed off as my teammates all looked at me. "Wait, you're seriously going with California's opinion?"

"Fact," West corrected, his tone mild. "Not opinion."

I opened my mouth to argue further, but Agnes lifted her hand to quiet me as Stuart read the next question.

"Wheesht, Maisie."

"But—"

"Wheesht."

"Fine," I muttered, crossing my arms over my chest, feeling like a child being chastised.

"The last question for quiz night is: In romantic stories, the appearance of a unicorn symbolizes what?"

West met my petulant gaze and smiled slowly.

"The nature of unicorns, often associated with immortality, is used to convey the idea of love enduring beyond time. Or, as romantics know it—true and everlasting love."

His perfectly precise tone and unwavering stare made my heart shiver, and warmth tingled through me as his words took hold.

"Finally, we have one bonus question in the spirit of Christmas," Stuart said, surprising us, and I turned my attention away from West to the man across the room. Bonus questions were rare, and often worth more points.

"Pay attention," I hissed, nudging West to look away from me. His stare was beginning to make me uncomfortable, as though he knew more about my inner workings than I did, and I wasn't quite sure what to do with the feelings that swirled inside of me.

"I can listen without looking at him," West assured me.

"What *local* legend is said to only occur during Christmas time?"

A delighted murmur rippled through the crowd, and I glared at West.

"Well, go on then, quizmaster. What is it, huh?" I raised my chin at West, ready for battle. There was no way he could know about our local legend. It was too small and inconsequential to have made its way into any story books.

"Stand down, soldier." West laughed. "Unfortunately, this falls outside my scope of knowledge."

"Ha!" I pointed my finger in the air and leaned closer to whisper. "It's the Christmas Wish at the standing stones, isn't it, Agnes?"

"It is." Agnes beamed.

"Now *that* sounds interesting. Tell me more." West looked between the two of us while Graham cleared his empty dishes.

"It's stupid." I sighed and tugged at a wayward lock of hair that had fallen over my shoulder. "It's said if you go to the stones and make a wish during the Christmas season then it will come true."

"It's not stupid," Agnes began. "It's magical and fun and—"

"Don't believe in magic?" West asked me, interrupting Agnes to focus on me.

"Absolutely not. If wishes came true, then—"

"Time's up," Hilda said at my shoulder, holding her hand out for our card. "The winner gets a sleigh ride. Well, if we get enough snow that is."

I dearly loved snow and was delighted to hear that we might win a sleigh ride. A farmer in the next village over offered rides with his pretty team of horses, and I'd always fancied taking one.

Fingers crossed, I settled in to await the scoring and ignored West's interested looks in my direction. Frankly, I didn't like his scrutiny. Maybe he just enjoyed our sparring. *Yes, that's what it is.* It's not my habit to seek the attraction of a tourist—*unlike Graham*—and despite his obvious good looks, I wasn't up for a fling with a random. That wasn't my MO at all, if I was honest.

"Drum roll please," Stuart called and began to read out the answers. When we got to the one about the chains and unicorn, and West was correct, I steadfastly ignored his gloating grin. *No, nope, no thank you.* I was not going to be attracted to this man's obvious intelligence. *No. Down girl.*

"Congratulations, you get to keep your crown," Stuart said to me, and the pub let out a collective groan while I jumped up and cheered.

Did I owe the win to West?
Maybe.
Was I going to admit that?
Nope.
I was taking my proverbial crown and going home.

CHAPTER THREE

Maisie

When I stepped out onto the street, thankful for another fun night—*and a win*—I was surprised to find that the clouds had cleared to reveal a full moon shimmering a trail of light across the dark waters of Loch Mirren. Thankful that I wouldn't have to fight the rain on my walk home, I turned the corner and strolled toward Agnes's flat where I was staying while I was in town helping her with the festival.

The Christmas Wish.

Such nonsense.

Restless, I continued past the flat, deciding that a walk in the crisp night air might clear my head. From a young age, I'd always had a busy brain, constantly fighting with sleep. Now, it wasn't uncommon for me to take long walks at night to untangle the thoughts that warred in my mind.

The curse of being a writer, I supposed.

Though I could hardly call myself that, could I? I

kicked at a rock on the pavement, sending it skittering toward the loch, and on impulse turned on a trail that led up a hill near the shoreline. The light from the moon was more than enough to illuminate my path, and I trundled along, lost in thought.

Thirty-three rejections.

The most recent had come just that morning, and I'd been in a foul mood all day because of it. For two years I'd queried literary agents and publishing houses alike, yet not a single one had been interested in my book. Quiz night had been the one bright spot in an otherwise annoying day, and now I couldn't even be fully happy about it because I knew that I hadn't been entirely responsible for our team's win. *Which was fine. Not everything falls on your shoulders, Maisie. You can let other people help.*

I'd still enjoy the win, even if I needed to share the kudos. If we got enough snow, then I'd be able to take the sleigh ride that I'd always wanted to go on but could never afford. I didn't blame the farmer for charging tourist prices for his sleigh rides. The season for snow was short here, as rain often washed it away, and he needed to make money for his business.

Dark shadows loomed in front of me on the hill and I stopped in my tracks, a shiver of apprehension making the fine hairs on the back of my neck stand up. When the shadows didn't move, I took a hesitant step forward, and then laughed at myself.

I'd somehow managed to find my way to the standing stones.

They looked pretty in the moonlight, I would give them that, and I walked closer to admire the way the stones jutted into the air, forming a circle atop the hill overlooking the shadowy loch below. Had this been a place of worship? Of ritual? For even a non-believer such as myself, I was hard-pressed to ignore the ambience of this moody setting. If I closed my eyes, I was half-convinced I'd hear the chants of ancient spells whispered across time.

Standing in the middle of the stones, I turned slowly in a full circle, admiring how the light from the moon coated the surrounding hills in a loving embrace. I'd never tire of living in Scotland, not when we had such beauty at our fingertips.

On impulse, I closed my eyes, bringing a wish to my mind.

While I didn't trust my future to the whims of magic, and as much as I dearly hoped that my book would get published, I couldn't bring myself to ask for what I wanted most. Instead, because I didn't *really* believe in this whole Christmas Wish legend anyway, I decided to wish for something simple and small.

"I wish for the snowiest Christmas *ever*," I said out loud, smiling as I imagined myself tucked on a sleigh with a team of prancing horses in front of me.

"I thought you didn't believe in magic."

I screeched and stumbled backward, tripping against a stone, and a hand grabbed my arm to steady me.

"West!" I exclaimed, glaring up at him. The moonlight glinted against his glasses, his lips quirking in that sexy half-smile, and my annoyance grew. *Of course* he'd find me here making a fool of myself. "You can't sneak up on women in the dark like that. You don't know my ninja skills. I could have karate-chopped your neck."

"Based on having to catch you before you fell over a stone, I'm suspecting I'm likely safe from your purported advanced defense mechanisms," West said.

Why, why *did I find his precise tone so hot?*

"Nevertheless, it's creepy to stalk a woman at night."

"I wasn't stalking. The stones hid your figure until I was closer. Your voice gave me a bit of a fright, I'll admit." West rocked back on his heels and looked down at me.

"Why are you up here?"

"I could ask the same of you."

"Must you be this frustrating?"

"Must you refuse to answer any questions asked of you?"

"I don't ... that's not ..." I furrowed my brow. Had I not answered his questions? I suppose I hadn't, but there was nothing in the rules that required me to answer questions from, well, anyone, really. "Maybe I don't feel like answering them."

"Why don't you just say that then?"

"Because it's rude?" I shook my head, just as a gust of wind sent a shiver down my back. I looked up at him in exasperation.

"I suspect offending others is not a top concern of yours."

"Hey!" I said, bringing a hand to my chest, mildly offended. "I do, somewhat, care about hurting other people's feelings."

"Offending people and hurting them are two different things. I suspect you care little what others think of you, but I didn't mean to imply that you were of a vicious nature. Though based on your competitive personality, I'm guessing you could attack if provoked." His mouth quirked that sexy smile, softening his words, and my heart danced.

Feigning anger, I held my hands up flat, as though I was going to karate chop him.

"Cease fire, my fair lady. I mean no harm." West held his own hands up in mock surrender and I was surprised when a giggle escaped. I was *so* not the type to giggle. Perhaps it was the ridiculousness of the situation, perched on the top of the hill under a full moon in the middle of an ancient circle of stones but, hey, at least I was no longer in a bad mood.

"I'll let you leave safely. *This* time." I made my tone menacing, and then stopped. "Wait, did you come here to make a wish?" Another gust of wind raced across the hills and West shivered. Reminding myself that he'd just come from California, I wondered if he'd brought proper cold weather gear with him.

"I made it." West gave me a look that sent a ripple of awareness through my body, and I had to bite my tongue before I asked what his wish had been. That was the way of wishes, wasn't it? They lost their power if you shared them.

"Well, best of luck to you and all that." I sniffed, turning to leave the circle of stones. By my estimation, the clouds gathering over the hills, which were beginning to crowd the stars, carried rain with them.

"Again, I find myself intrigued. Weren't you the one *just* insisting that you didn't believe in magic?"

"I don't," I said, pushing past him to storm back down the hill. To my surprise, he hooked his arm through mine and stopped my advance. Slowly, he brought me to his side, so we were arm in arm as we walked. I didn't need the support, but a part of me liked how he handled me so effortlessly. It hadn't even been a question for him, this need to escort me. Perhaps West was a man driven by manners and rules, which tracked with the whole buttoned-up scholarly vibe I was getting from him.

"Methinks you're a liar."

I snorted, amused despite myself.

"I don't believe wishes come true. If they did … well, I'm just saying that things would have been different for me is all."

"Why? What wishes haven't come true for you?" West stopped me, and I turned, my mouth working as he studied me seriously, as though my answer was the most important thing in the world. Who *was* this man? He didn't get a glimpse behind the curtain at my dreams and failures, that was for certain, and I narrowed my eyes at him.

"A touch presumptuous, wouldn't you say? I barely know you," I said, my breath catching as he leaned a touch closer. Was he going to kiss me? The shock of it stilled me, a thrill zipping through me, and I felt something crackle in the air around us, like energy building during a lightning storm.

"Is it?" West considered my words carefully, as though he actually cared about my thoughts. "In that case, I suppose it would be even more presumptuous to ask you for a kiss."

"A … what?" I'd been *right*. Excitement danced, causing my skin to heat, and once more a foolish giggle worked through me, threatening to bubble up. Which was so not like me, and yet, there was something about this man that put me on my back foot.

"A kiss. A smooch. A peck. A snog, if you're British, I believe. Categorically known as a sign for exhibiting attraction for another person, a kiss is typically shared by caressing our lips together."

Could someone both annoy and excite me? Because this man was managing to do it in the same breath. Yes, I wanted to kiss him, even if just to stop his proper recitation of what a kiss was. As though I didn't know the actual definition of a kiss. When the corner of his lips quirked, just shy of a smile, I understood he was teasing me.

"Is this your way of hitting on a woman?" I shifted on my feet, my interest piqued. "By lecturing them on the definition of a kiss?"

"Typically, no. We'd already be kissing at this point. But your question indicated confusion, and therefore I thought it would—"

Frustrated that he was forcing me to say it, because *yes*, I very much did want to kiss this strange, sexy, buttoned-up man, I hooked an arm around his neck and pulled his head down to mine. Pressing my lips against his, I closed my eyes as a rush of emotion flooded me.

I'd never been one to dream of my wedding or the perfect man for me. While other wee girls made scrapbooks or talked about their perfect wedding one day, I'd been lost in books about dragons or hidden worlds stuck behind faery doors in the forest. My favorite were the stories where the princess rescued herself, and so, no, I'd never much thought about finding *the* one for me.

West angled his head, taking control of the kiss as his arms came around me, and something seemed to shift inside me. It was an understanding, as easily as I knew that I loved eighties music and hated brussels sprouts, that this was a man who had the power to change the trajectory of my future. This knowledge rattled me, and I clenched my hand into the thick jumper he wore, shaken by the truth that stirred in my soul.

I should push him away.

Instead, I pulled him closer, his kiss sweeping me under. He tasted of mint and impulsive decisions, and the combination heated my blood. A gust of wind skated icicles down my neck, cooling my warm skin, and I eased back, breaking the kiss.

"I knew it," West said, and I cocked my head at him as I worked to bring my breathing under control.

"Knew what?" I asked, turning to see the dark storm clouds had edged closer.

"It's you."

The way he regarded me, like I was a gift to be unwrapped, was unsettling. I'd never been looked at like that before. *Was that a thrill of anticipation I felt? Was that even a thing?*

"Care to explain?" I asked, nerves forcing me to stumble forward down the hill. West hooked my arm, steadying me, and my heart raced as I focused one foot in front of the other.

"The woman I've been waiting my whole life for."

I mean, I *knew* I was a good kisser, but I'd yet to have a man fall head over heels into love after just a taste. I gave West the side-eye, even though my heart wanted to betray me and dance out of my chest at his words.

"First time in Scotland?" I asked, brushing his declaration aside.

"Yes."

"Och, well, that'll do it. Scotland's a very romantic place." I swept my hand out to indicate the moonlight shimmering on the loch, the dark hills silhouetted in the distance. "Castles, stunning landscapes, standing stones ... it's easy to get carried away."

"No," West stated, his voice steady. "I don't get carried away."

"Come on, West. Everyone gets carried away once in a while."

"Not me. I'm very methodical. In *everything* that I do." His voice turned husky, the warm timbre of it and the undeniable meaning of his words heating my core. I had to tamp down the baser side of myself that wanted to take him up on his unspoken promise.

"I—"

A flash of light caught my eye, and I froze.

A highland coo, a very *transparent* highland coo, mind you, sprung from a bush in front of us, with one leg lifted, as though to say, "ta-da!"

I'd always thought I'd be the person who handled ghosts with fearless aplomb and make all the right choices, unlike a character in a scary movie.

Turns out I, too, lose my cool when a ghost jumps out of nowhere in front of my face.

On a shriek, I twisted to run and was shocked to find my feet no longer on the ground.

"Nooooo!" I scrambled, my feet flailing in the air, before I registered that West had scooped me up in one smooth motion and was calmly carrying me down the hillside. I wrangled in his arms like a cat trying to escape its bath, certain that the demon coo would be chasing us down the hill. "Hurry, hurry, hurry, hurry." I chanted the word on refrain, wrapping my arms around West's shoulders, panic making me cling to him tighter.

"It's okay, love, we're almost at the road."

Love?

The man must be mental. That was it. The holidays were clearly getting to everyone. I'd been silly enough to make a wish at the standing stones. West was drunk on Scotland's romance, or maybe just drunk, and we'd both managed to see a ghost coo. I'd have to speak to Graham about cleaning his tap lines. Perhaps there was a weird mold that was making people hallucinate.

"Mooooo!"

The ghost coo jumped in front of us again, clearly a fan of the ol' jump scare, and bellowed in our faces. West's grip momentarily slipped, but I was stuck to him like a barnacle on a ship.

"I think … the ghost is … having fun?" West whispered, his breath hot at my ear, and despite my fear, my toes curled at the brush of his lips on my sensitive skin.

"You can see him then? It's not just me?"

"Which ghost did you think I was referring to, Maisie?" West asked, and I wanted to snarl at him.

"Moo!" This time, the coo shuffled forward, his outburst a short bark, and I realized that West might be right.

"It's like being haunted by a six-year-old who thinks fart jokes are funny," West declared.

The coo's face fell, if that was even possible, and his furry shoulders slumped.

"And I, for one, *love* fart jokes, don't you, Maisie?" West quickly amended, seeing the change of stature in the ghost.

Oh, so now we were reassuring the ghost that he was ghosty enough? Ghostful? Ghostical? Shaking my head, I looked between the coo and West, unable to speak.

"Best ghost I've seen all night," West promised the coo, and it perked up, doing a little shimmy before disappearing from sight.

"I can't believe that just happened." My heart drummed in my chest and I forced myself to ease the tight grip I had on West.

"Where am I delivering you?" West asked, walking toward town with me still in his arms while I gaped up at him. The first drops of rain started, and I made a move to get out of West's grasp, but he just hugged me closer.

"I can walk, you know," I grumbled. Begrudgingly, I pointed the way. I would not admit that I was still rattled, and it felt good to be cradled close like I was the most important thing in the world to him.

"But this is nicer, don't you think?" West stopped in front of Agnes's flat, which was attached to her bookstore, and looked down at me. A drop of rain hit his forehead, and despite myself, I reached up and brushed it away.

"Thank you, erm, for the ride," I said as West lowered me to the ground but kept his arms locked around me. "West, I—"

"Will you have dinner with me?"

"I don't think I can. The festival is only days away and I've promised to help." I wasn't brushing him off, we truly had a ton of work to do to finish getting ready for the festival, but a part of me also needed to take a step back before I lost my head and agreed to date this incredibly handsome stranger.

"How can I help?"

"Oh, I'm sure we've got it handled. It's just busy is all. Agnes is running me ragged."

"So, it's Agnes I'll need to ask how to help then." West's lips quirked. I was torn between wanting to take him upstairs and have my way with him and running far, far, away before he changed my life forever.

"West." It was a plea.

Understanding, West stepped back and turned to go. My body felt cold from his absence, and my stomach turned, watching him leave.

"Maisie." West turned back and looked down at me, his handsome face serious. "Do you not feel this? Am I reading this wrong? Because if so, I'll back off. I'm not one to make a woman feel uncomfortable if she's not wanting the attention."

I pressed my lips together, my heart sighing at his kindness, because I understood, to my core, that he was a good man. Sure, he was pressing me about seeing me, but the fact that he'd even cared to ask, already worried for my comfort, was enough to make me let my walls down ... a bit.

"I'll admit there's an interest." I angled my head at him, a touch coy.

"And do I have your permission to pursue said interest?" West perked up.

"Why, my good sir, are you asking to court me?" I affected a stiff, upper crust accent.

"Perhaps I am, milady, perhaps I am." West mirrored my accent, and I forced down a laugh.

"Then I'll see you tomorrow at the bookstore."

Before I could stop him, West snatched my hand and kissed it lavishly, and I laughed outright as the skies opened. Unperturbed, West sauntered away, whistling a jaunty tune.

What had I gotten myself into?

Shaking my head, I raced upstairs, got ready for bed, and dove under the covers. My head was spinning. Had I ever had a day that contained so many mixed emotions? Rejection, frustration, joy, shock … *delight.* I wasn't sure I'd sleep having had such a contradictory day, but it wasn't long before I drifted into the first contented sleep I'd had in months.

CHAPTER FOUR

West

"Yoooo-hooo."

A banging at my cottage door jolted me awake, and I blinked at the wooden beams crossing the ceiling while my brain tried to recalibrate my location.

Scotland.

That's right. Jumping out of bed, I reached for my glasses on the side table and put them on, before padding to the front door of the cottage. It was far too cold for me to sleep in just shorts as I preferred, so at least I was partially clothed when I pulled the door open to a group of grandmotherly type women, all with curious expressions on their faces as they looked me up and down.

"My, my, my." One woman pursed her lips and put a hand on her hip, fluttering her eyelashes at me, and my eyebrows raised to my hairline.

"Good morning, ladies. Can I help you?"

"Did we get you out of bed?" Another woman, this one

wearing a sweatshirt that read *I will Dewey Decimate you,* gave me a disapproving look.

"Ah, yes, it seems you did. I just flew in from California yesterday, so I'm afraid the time difference is something I'll need to adjust to. How can I be of service, ladies?"

What I dearly needed was to brush my teeth and mainline coffee for at least an hour while I obsessed over the memory of Maisie's lips on mine.

"An American. I hope you're here for the book festival?" This grandmother's sweatshirt read *Mind if I check you out?* alongside an image of a library book.

"Yes, partly. Ladies, please, if you could tell me how I can be of assistance?"

"Stop ogling the man and ask him for help, Esther." This woman's sweatshirt stated that she liked big books and could not lie. I was sensing a theme here.

"I knew we should've taken my car."

"My car is perfectly fine," Dewey Decimate barked.

"Car troubles?" I guessed, crossing my arms against the morning's brisk chill.

"Flat tire. And none of us feel like getting dirty." Esther, I presumed, nodded at me.

"Well, at least you're honest." I laughed and gestured them inside against the sharp gust of wind that buffeted across the grey waters of Loch Mirren. "Let me just get dressed and I'm happy to help."

"Thank you so much. I'm Meredith, and this is Esther, Cherise, and Shannon. Lila couldn't make it. We're the Book Bitches from Kingsbarns." Meredith said this last part as though I should be suitably impressed, so I made an approving sound.

Esther snorted.

"Stop trying to show off, Meredith. The lad will never have heard of us. Your own cousin hasn't heard of our book club," Esther said, walking into the kitchen and pulling out the empty coffee pot. I raised an eyebrow at her audacity but then realized that I wasn't the least bit bothered with these ladies making themselves at home in my rental kitchen. If they wanted to put coffee on while I dressed, I wasn't going to stop them.

"But we had a video go viral on Booktok," Cherise said, dropping onto a stool at the counter. The women began to argue the merits of their fame and I faded into the bedroom, closing the door gently behind me, surprised to find myself fighting a grin. Even though I'd come here for peace and quiet, thinking a book festival in Scotland would lend itself to restful afternoons of reading, I'd barely had a moment to myself since I'd arrived.

Not that any of *that* mattered anymore.

I'd found her.

The one.

My dream girl, tucked away in a small village in Scotland, all sharp edges and soft curves, moody eyes and biting words. Maybe it was my sleep-addled brain, or maybe it was my penchant for believing in fairy tales, but something had clicked inside me the moment I'd laid my eyes upon Maisie. It was more than just lust, or an instant attraction to a pretty woman in a pub. No, this was a deep-rooted understanding that if I handed this woman my heart, she'd hold the power to shatter it into a million pieces. I only had to decide if Maisie was worth the risk. Well. Not only that. We lived on opposite sides of the world, so I had to decide if I *should* want to try.

I wanted to convince her to date me, but the rational part of my brain—the one that most often dictated my life—was warring against that. Perhaps it was the crisp air here, or perhaps it was my attraction to her, but I was determined to woo Maisie. Having promised courtship, anything less than that was unacceptable. Which meant I would show up at the shop to help today and do my best to get closer to Maisie. Although, glancing at my phone, I'd be a bit late. Hurrying, I made use of the bathroom, dressed, and by the time I returned to the kitchen, the Book Bitches were enjoying a cup of coffee, two seated at the breakfast bar and two on the couch.

"We poured you a cup but weren't sure how you took it." Meredith nodded to the cup on the counter.

"Thank you." Crossing the room, I inhaled half a cup of coffee, my brain finally shuddering awake, as the women chattered excitedly about the festival. An idea formed.

"Ladies, what kind of books did you say you like to read?"

"We, of course, read *all* subject matters," Cherise, of the Dewey Decimate shirt, promised me.

"I like the smut books," Esther said, her tastes seemingly in line with her "check you out" shirt.

"We *all* like the smut books." Meredith smiled at me when I grinned. "Smut, romance, closed-door, bad-boy, sweet romance ... we'll take them all. But periodically, we veer off course into a nice grisly thriller when the mood strikes."

"We don't judge," Shannon assured me.

"Even better. Ladies after my own heart." Leaning against the counter, I crossed my feet at my ankles and poured the last of the pot into my cup. "I'm a literature professor, and I have a particular love for fairy tales."

"Are you married?" Esther demanded and my grin widened.

"Nope."

"How old are you?" Shannon asked, fluttering her eyelashes.

"Too young for you, hussy." Meredith turned to Shannon and sniffed.

"What? We read age-gap romances," Shannon protested.

"As such, I'm hoping you'll help be my fairy godmothers of sorts," I said quickly, drawing their attention away from debating the merits of my marketability as a love interest.

"I like the sound of this," Esther said. Leaning forward, she squinted at me. "Go on."

"I met the woman of my dreams last night. However, it's been brought to my attention that I will need to court her, if you will, and I'd like to do so, perhaps with your assistance?"

Squeals greeted my announcement, and the questions came fast and furious.

"Who is she?"

"Is she a princess? Courting sounds so formal."

"Where did you meet her?"

"Should we kidnap her?"

At that, everyone turned to look at Esther, who shrugged innocently.

"What? It's one way to guarantee her attention."

"I'd prefer to refrain from any international crimes, if at all possible," I stressed, putting my cup down on the counter. "I'm meant to go to the bookshop today to offer my assistance with helping at the festival. Maisie will be there, and I'd like to convince her to have dinner with me."

"Have you tried asking?" Shannon narrowed her eyes at me.

"Of course, he's asked her. He's not dumb." Meredith turned and glared at me. "You asked the girl already, didn't you?"

"I did. She was ... interested, but I didn't get a solid yes from her."

"Got it. All right, ladies! We have a quest. Volunteer at the Book Festival and Operation True Love." Meredith stood and clapped her hands together.

"What if it's not true love?" Cherise asked, bringing the empty cups to the kitchen. At least the rental had been stocked with coffee, I thought, happy now that the caffeine was humming in my system.

"Don't they deserve the chance to figure that out together?" Esther asked.

"That's fair. We'll have to discuss strategies." The women began arguing with each other as they piled out the front door and I hastily grabbed my keys, phone, and jacket. I'd actually just changed my roommate's tire a few weeks prior, so I was confident I could get them on the road quickly. But, with the way the wind seemed to want to slice me open with its icy blades of fury, I was also hoping they'd give me a ride into town after. At some point, I would need to sort out groceries, but for now, I just wanted to see Maisie again.

By the time I had the tire changed, with much fanfare and a few "my heroes" thrown about, we were on our way into Loren Brae. I'd been positioned in the middle of the backseat, and we'd been delayed five minutes while the Book Bitches fought over who got to sandwich me. Once that was sorted, we arrived at Bonnie Books in no time, and I got my first look at Loren Brae in the daylight.

The cheerful village hugged the frigid waters of Loch Mirren, colorful buildings tumbling on top of each other, each door painted a different color. It was as though the town had been built as an afterthought, each building attaching to the next, and it reminded me of the hodgepodge nature of the pub and how all the pieces jumbled together to form a perfect picture. Bonnie Books was a hive of activity, with people streaming in and out of a stone building with pretty, arched windows that looked out over the loch. It was a space for dreamers. How did anyone visit here and remain unaffected? I stepped out of the car, the Book Bitches' chatter fading behind me, as I caught a glimpse of Maisie through the tall front window. She was laughing, her hands full of books, her hair wild around her head, and I stopped, a ripple of understanding moving through me. I wanted to be the one she smiled at like that.

"That's the girl?" Esther asked at my elbow, and I nodded, not taking my eyes off Maisie.

"That's the one."

The words were a truth balm to my soul, soothing a heart that had worried I'd be lonely forever, and I took a deep breath to steady myself.

"I say we badger her until she agrees to go out with you."

"We can guilt her into it."

"Yes! Shame her for not taking a chance on this fine man."

"I have rope in the boot ..."

At that, I rounded on the women.

"No kidnapping. No force. No badgering. If you can't find a way to be subtle about your matchmaking, then I'm relieving you of your quest." I gave the women my sternest look while using my professor lecture voice.

"What about us suggests we have a knack for subtlety?" Esther barked out a laugh.

The woman had a point.

"We'll be on our best behavior. Promise. Wouldn't want to scare off the lass now, would we?" Meredith rubbed her hands together like she was about to dive into a chocolate cake.

I hoped I wouldn't regret my invitation to engage this army of book grandmothers to a task that I desperately hoped wouldn't be as monumental as they were making it out to be.

Maisie turned, having deposited the books on a table, and caught sight of us outside the window. A smile bloomed on her face and then she made great show of looking at her watch and shaking her head. Making a mental note to set my alarm for the next day, I walked through the door of Bonnie Books.

And into chaos.

The front of the building belied the sheer size of the bookshop, and much like everything in this town it seemed, more was revealed the deeper you looked. Agnes had set the shop up in what resembled small gathering areas, with chairs and bookshelves scattered about and moody art lining the walls. A conversation area, with large floor pillows scattered in front of a fire that crackled merrily, held a group of women who were working on decorations.

"Good afternoon. Have yourself a lie-in then?" Maisie turned to me. A startled expression crossed her face a half-second before she careened into me, and I caught her against my chest before she fell.

"Goodness, I am *so* clumsy," Esther purred, holding a hand to her chest. Maisie blinked at the dainty grandmother who had just hip-checked her with all the aplomb of a linebacker. "Caught my foot on the rug."

"Are you okay?" I smiled softly down at Maisie as she turned back to me, her eyes catching and hesitating on mine. Her mouth opened, just a bit, and I had to fight not to lean down for a taste. Just as I'd remembered from the night before, she fit perfectly into my arms, and I didn't want to let her go.

"Um, yes, I am. Thanks." At Maisie's gentle tug, I released her, wondering if she felt the same shiver of excitement where our bodies had touched. Maisie turned and I shot Esther a warning look. She studiously ignored me to examine the spine of a book she'd picked up. "Make some new friends?"

"Of course, he did. Would you look at the man? He was beating the women off him. We rescued him, is what we did." Cherise leaned in and winked. "Though, to be honest, we kind of wanted him for ourselves."

"Is that right?" Maisie asked, amusement lighting her face.

"You may be younger than me, darling, but with age comes wisdom. And I've learned a lot," Cherise said, tapping the cover of a romance novel she'd picked up that depicted a man in a pirate costume holding a woman whose bosom barely stayed in her dress. She gave Maisie a knowing look to make certain that Maisie understood her competition.

"Maisie, these are the Book Bitches of Kingsbarns, who have descended upon the town like a plague or blessing, depending on how you care to interpret it," I said, silently laughing as Meredith glared at me. "As you can ascertain, they are here to offer their assistance in your time of need. Please, put them to work. The more tedious, the better."

"The Book Bitches!" Agnes appeared, looking like a bright-eyed candy cane in a red and white striped sweater, and beamed at the group of grandmothers. "I've heard so much about you ladies. Isn't it true you helped Graham's cousin get the Royal Unicorn up and running again? How's it getting on then?"

"It's grand," Meredith said, delighted that someone had finally acknowledged their fame. "The pub's running along neatly, and our wee war kitten has his own Instagram account now."

"Naturally," Agnes agreed, bending over the phone Meredith pulled out. The women walked away to discuss cats that went to war, apparently, while I tried to stand as close to Maisie as I could without being creepy.

"I'm sorry I'm late. I should have set an alarm to account for the time difference."

"Nae bother." Maisie beckoned for me to follow her to a table where a pile of posters and markers were stacked. Picking up a flier, she handed it to me. A tingle danced up my hand when her fingers brushed mine. *What was with this instant, visceral reaction I have every time I touch her?* I felt like I was sixteen again, all unchecked hormones and nervous energy, and all I needed was for my voice to crack to give away my obvious attraction. "So, while it is a Christmas Book Festival, the theme isn't solely focused on Christmas. We've partnered with local artisans who will also sell their wares and holiday gifts, but we've focused this year's theme on mood reading."

"Mood reading?" I took the flier she gave me and read out some of the text. "*Books that make you miss home. Books to curl up with by a fire. Cozy books for cold nights. Books that make you believe in love.* Ah, sure, I get it now. So will each stall have books that fall into a particular vibe?"

"Exactly. We'll have them at the stalls, as well as at the stores and the pub. For example, Agnes wanted the pub's mood to be books that make you give up women and become a monk, but we vetoed her."

"What does Graham get then?" I asked, enjoying the banter between this group of friends.

"Books that make you want to celebrate."

"Slightly more fitting, I'm sure."

"Much to Agnes's annoyance, yes."

"How can I help?" *Please say something that involves me working closely with you.*

"You can either help with making the signs for each shop or with moving the actual books to the stores."

I glanced around the room at the shop filled predominantly with women and quickly determined that moving the books would be an easier task for me. I didn't want any of the Book Bitches to try and lift something too heavy for them to carry. Though, with the way Esther had hip-checked Maisie, they were likely stronger than they looked. I followed Maisie to a room tucked off the back with high ceilings and a tall window that looked out over a cobble-stoned side street. A dog wandered past, and concern grew until I saw an old man hobbling along the pavement, the dog waiting patiently at the corner for him.

"That's Mr. Thompson. He's got Colin to keep him company on his walks." Maisie came to stand by my side, as we watched the man stroll along.

"I was worried the dog was on its own."

"No, he's well looked after, that one. Spoiled, really. He walks every day, rain or shine, and Colin sees that he gets home safe."

"That's sweet." She stood close, her shoulder almost touching mine, and I glanced down at her. Maisie darted a shy look up at me, her cheeks tinging pink, and I took the opportunity of us being alone to remind her about the night before.

"You never did tell me what you really wanted to wish for." I'd heard her wish about the snow for Christmas, but she hadn't shared what her secret wish was. A storm cloud crossed Maisie's face, and she turned to the long tables piled high with books.

"Boxes are there. Books are sorted into piles with their labels."

"Maisie," I said, catching her arm as she turned and stopping her. I kept my voice soft. "I want to get to know you, but if it makes you uncomfortable, you don't have to answer my questions."

"It's stupid, really." Maisie pulled away and began assembling a cardboard box. She shook her head with a half laugh, her curls tumbling about as she pulled out some packing tape. "And it's not a secret. Maybe I just don't want to share it with you because I'm afraid you'll think less of me."

"Unless you're about to tell me that you've killed a man and sewed his skin into a Christmas hat, I don't think there's much you can say that will rattle me." I laughed at Maisie's horrified look. "Maisie, I'm a professor of literature at one of the most progressive universities in the United States. When I tell you that my students have told me every story known to man, they have. There's not much you'll say that will shock me."

"You're a professor of literature?" Maisie put her hands on her hips and gaped at me.

"Yes. Why did you think that I knew so much about Scottish mythology?"

"That explains the voice," Maisie said, tapping a finger to her lips.

"The voice?"

"Your voice. It's like all ... precise. And modulated. And dignified." Maisie shook her shoulders and walked around like she was a penguin, apparently meaning to look distinguished.

"I do *not* walk like that."

"No. But you talk like that."

"If that's your estimation, I certainly can't ..." I trailed off as I heard my own voice. Sighing, I scrubbed a hand across my face, amusement lighting inside me, as I moved to the table and began to box books for a cozy evening by the fire. "I suppose that's fair."

"Do you write?" Maisie cast me a look from where she returned to boxing books next to me.

"I dabble. I haven't quite worked up the courage for a full book. Yet. Just short stories, poetry, and some amusing bits here and there." I shrugged, at peace with it. There was something inside me that understood that the right story would come to me at the right time.

"I do, too. Write, that is." Maisie continued to stack the books, even though there was a tremulous note in her voice.

"Really? That's great. What do you write?"

"A novel. Well, novels, now. Cozy who-dun-it style. But modernized. Kind of like Agatha Christie meets Sex in the City."

"That sounds incredible," I said, turning to her with delight only to see her face fall.

"Apparently not," Maisie bit out, her face sad.

"What's wrong, Maisie? Was that your wish?" I stopped what I was doing and turned to her, understanding that whatever was happening here was the crux of her issues.

"No, not really. I wouldn't wish something so important at the standing stones," Maisie grumbled, revealing her vulnerability.

"Maisie, finishing a novel is a huge accomplishment in itself. Most people never even get that far. You should be proud of yourself. It's truly an amazing feat," I said, reaching out to tilt her face up to mine.

"Yeah, well, thirty-three rejections say otherwise."

We both jumped as the door slammed, a resounding

click indicating the lock being thrown. I rolled my eyes to the ceiling as Maisie raced to the door and tried it.

"It's locked," Maisie said, looking down at the handle in surprise. Knocking, she called out for attention.

While cheesy, and an obvious ploy to lock us in a room together, I decided maybe the Book Bitches had read enough romance novels that this might work in my favor. Glancing around the room, my eyes lit on the Christmas decorations.

"Let me try." I came to stand beside her and jiggled the handle and tugged a few times, knowing it was futile.

"Bloody hell," Maisie said. She raised her fist to pound, but I grabbed it in my hand, grinning when she looked at me in confusion. Then I let my eyes trail upwards, and she followed my gaze. "Oh."

"Are you a follower of traditions?" I asked, my eyes on the mistletoe hanging directly above our heads.

"Not really." Maisie sniffed in disdain.

"Ah, fair enough," I said, moving to turn away, and almost laughed out loud at Maisie's crestfallen expression.

"Wait, I mean ... I suppose we wouldn't want to bring any bad luck upon ourselves."

"No, best not to." Warmth filled me as I nudged her until her back was pressed flat against the door and braced my hands on either side of her shoulders, caging her in. Dipping my head, I brought my mouth close to her ear. "You smell like cinnamon. I wonder if you'll taste the same."

Maisie exhaled softly, trembling slightly as I trailed my lips lightly across her neck and up to her mouth, sinking into the kiss. I stayed right there, not touching her except with my mouth, bracing myself against the door as Maisie moaned against my lips. She bucked against me, and I deepened the kiss, desire flaring at Maisie's reaction. Her exterior may be prickly, but her response was heated, and she reached up and ran her hands across my chest to my back, pulling me closer to her body. Once again, I noticed how well we fit together and pressed her tightly against the door.

Hunger licked between us, and she opened her mouth, tasting, and moaned. It was the moan that did me in. Dropping my hands to her waist, I hitched her up, so her legs wound around me, and pressed her back against the door once more, sinking into her softness.

The doorknob jiggled.

"Is this locked?" Agnes called, and we broke apart. Slowly, I slid Maisie down my body, our eyes caught, our chests heaving with barely restrained need.

"Well, I think, um, we're lucky and all that ..." Maisie mumbled, pink tinging her cheeks, before she raced across the room and resumed packing a box. When the door opened a crack, and Agnes peered inside, I caught it with my hand before it hit me in the face.

"Yes, it was locked. Thanks for letting us out," I said.

"That's the weirdest thing," Agnes said, turning in confusion. I looked over her head to see the Book Bitches watching me from across the room. With Agnes's back turned, I lifted my hand and gave them a thumbs up.

"Told ya," Esther said, slapping Cherise's shoulder. "Now we just need to kidnap the girl."

CHAPTER FIVE

Maisie

"Yooo-hooo, dear?"

I veered away from the main room of the bookstore after I'd come inside from taking the rubbish out to the bin and poked my head into the storage room. There, I found the Book Bitches caught in chaos. Or creating chaos. I wasn't quite sure if chaos followed them, or they manifested it, but thus far today they'd managed to simultaneously help and derail many of our efforts. I sensed another such catastrophe headed my way as I surveyed where the women stood, strands of Christmas lights tangled around them.

"Och, you've gone and mucked things up now, haven't you?" If I recalled correctly, the lights had been neatly packed away when I'd last seen them.

"It's not our fault that the lights weren't properly

stored. Everyone knows it's almost impossible to pack these strands correctly." Meredith glared at me, like I'd been the one to come in here and single-handedly knot all the strands together.

"Twistie-ties." Shannon nodded sagely at me. "That's the best method for keeping them from tangling."

"Or hanging them from a clothes hook," Cherise said, handing me a massive bundle. "Here, dear. Hold these while we try to untangle them."

"But," I said, straining to see over the large ball of lights in my arms. "This is massive. Surely it will take hours to unravel."

"Best to get started now then," Esther assured me, tugging at a strand from the ball. "Here, take this end, Cherise."

Cherise took one end and looped around me.

"Meredith, can you grab this?"

"No, Shannon, look here's another end," Meredith said.

"Wait, ladies," I began, feeling the cords wrapping around my back and my legs. I could barely see over the mess in my arms. "You're getting me caught."

"Stop. You're doing it wrong," Cherise insisted.

"No, it's this way. Grab this end," Shannon said. The women danced around me, arguing, as trepidation grew inside me. I could feel the cords winding around my legs and my waist and my anxiety kicked up.

"That's enough," I ordered.

"What's enough?" West appeared at the door. Not that I could see him through the growing ball of lights in my arms, but his voice was clear. "Oh dear. Didn't we talk about this?"

"Talk about what?" I demanded.

"West, can you hold this?" one of the women asked. I could no longer make out who was speaking and cursed under my breath when someone bumped into me from behind.

"Ladies, stand down," West ordered, using a no-nonsense tone that gave me a funny shiver of recognition. "You can't just tether me to Maisie."

"Did they get you caught up in this too?" I tried to take a step forward and someone bumped against me again.

"Don't move," West said, his voice much closer now. "They've managed to tie my legs to yours."

Oh. It took everything in my power not to think about being tied to West, in decidedly different circumstances. Even so, his nearness was causing my skin to heat.

"Would you look at the time? We're late for our tea."

"Must get on with it. Time for a cuppa."

"Back in a bit."

The women's voices disappeared behind the telltale sound of a door slamming shut, and I sighed. My arms were beginning to tremble from holding this awkward ball of lights.

"Do you think I can put this down? My arms are beginning to tire." West surveyed my very full arms.

"Hold on. Let me see." There was motion at my back and then West's arms came around my waist, lifting the ball from my hands. I shivered as his hard body pressed into my back, looming over me, and at just how right his arms felt around my waist. "Can you shuffle forward a bit so we can put this down at the table? Then I can get to unwinding us.

They certainly managed to get you well and truly tangled, didn't they?"

"You could say that. A bit chaotic, aren't they?"

"Like a hurricane on a sunny spring day." West's breath was warm at my neck, and I laughed as we shuffled slowly forward, his thighs nudging the backs of my legs. Warmth pooled low, and a delicious ache of desire tugged at my core.

"There. Let's put it down, then I'm going to turn back around and see how I can start unraveling this mess."

"Right. On you go then."

West dropped the ball on the table, and it landed with a soft plop, several strands still connected around me. I bit down on a giggle, as West cursed, wobbling at my back as he attempted to turn and step his legs out of the strands.

"Oh no!" West cried, a second before the cords pulled tight and I toppled to the floor with him. Well, I didn't land on the floor. But it might as well have been for the lack of softness on West's body. Somehow, he'd managed to twist so he cradled me against his chest, his arms cushioning me. And even more miraculously, I hadn't heard any broken lights being crushed beneath us. Tilting my head up, I broke out in laughter at the mutinous look on his face.

"You don't look so pleased to have me in your arms."

"*That* particular circumstance I'm delighted with. My preferred manner would be to get you there of your own desires, not because you've been, literally, roped into it."

At his precise tone and clear annoyance with the Book Bitches, my laughter rocketed, and soon we were both howling on the floor, clutching each other.

"Maybe they'll find us here one day, long forgotten in

the back of the bookstore, skeletons wrapped in Christmas lights."

"One certainly hopes that they won't leave us to perish." West shifted, bringing his hand up to cup my chin, and tilted my face toward him. "Have I told you how breathtaking you are?"

My heart fluttered in my chest, a butterfly about to take flight.

"Is that because I'm currently crushing your chest and rendering you unable to breathe?" I aimed for lightness, hoping to ease the tension of the moment. Otherwise, I might lose my mind and do something like have my way with this man on the floor of a stockroom.

Which would most definitely get me a lump of coal in my Christmas stocking.

"There's a type of Iris that has these velvety black petals on the outside which resembles your hair. But the center of the flower is the prettiest, deepest blue, like your gorgeous eyes. You remind me of it."

Now *I* was the one out of breath. I couldn't remember anyone ever comparing me to a flower before, at least not in such a manner. He studied me like I was a painting done by one of the grand masters, a piece of art to be admired, and I had no frame of reference for how to handle something, no *someone*, like this. Here I thought I'd wade into the waters, perhaps have a little holiday fling, and now I found myself out of my depth.

"We'd, um, we'd better get out of this mess before Agnes realizes we're missing." I cleared my throat, desperately wanting to kiss him again. But without the adrenaline from the other night coursing through my veins, and the rules of mistletoe dictating my actions, nerves made me strangely hesitant to do so. He shifted immediately, respecting my words, and rolled me to the side so we both half-sat on our bums while we began to unravel the cords from around our legs. The silence drew out, making me uncomfortable, so I jumped to the first topic that popped into my head.

"Will you be going to the gingerbread house competition at the pub tonight?"

West laughed, tilting his head at me in surprise.

"Do I look like the type to compete in a gingerbread house competition?"

"It's hard to say. Fergus from the sheep farm has won the last two years."

"Is that right? In that case, I'd be hard-pressed to say no. If you're asking me to come along that is?"

Nerves twisted my stomach. While I hadn't worked up the courage to kiss him again, I still wanted to spend more time with him. I took great care in focusing on a strand of lights wrapped around my ankle.

"If you'd like to join me, it could be fun."

"It's a date then." West grinned when I flashed him a look of annoyance. Wasn't he the one who was supposed to be wooing me? As if reading my mind, his grin widened.

"I'd planned to ask you to dinner tonight, but this sounds much more entertaining. I can't wait to see the type of gingerbread structure that a man named Fergus creates."

"A barn," I muttered, finally freeing my ankle. "The man is partial to barns."

"A gingerbread barn. This I have to see."

"He's quite good at it. It's a fierce competition." I

narrowed my eyes at West. "Don't be getting any ideas about us working together on one. I already have my own plans. You'll have to crack on with your own design."

West held a hand to his chest.

"I would never seek to impede your chance for glory."

I couldn't help myself, and I laughed, bending to work on my other ankle.

"There's that voice again. It's like you're giving a lecture. But, without being all lecture-y."

"Is lecture-y a word?" West stood and kicked his legs free, bending to gather some of the strands that had come loose on the floor.

"Are ghost coos real?" I countered, freeing my other ankle. I accepted the hand he held out to me and stood.

"Lecture-y it is then." West pushed his glasses up on his nose. "It has been pointed out to me on occasion that my profession has seeped over into my day-to-day vernacular."

"It's hot." The words were out before I could stop them, and my breath left my body when he stepped close enough to kiss me. The man towered over me, and I had to crane my neck to look up at him.

"I have it on good authority that when a woman utters an expression such as this that she is, at the very least, displaying a modicum of interest in the receiver of said phrase. Would I be correct in said assessment of your words?" West lowered his glasses and gave me a cheeky wink.

"Be still my heart, *Professor*." I fanned my face, pretending to be dizzy, and West laughed, wrapping his arms around my waist. My heart stilled when he brushed the softest of kisses across my mouth, like a snowflake melting on my lips, and then pulled away.

"Surely the women don't expect us to untangle these strands? We'll be here for days."

"I think these are just backup. If I'm correct, Agnes had the lights strung yesterday."

"Good, let's play hooky. I'll treat you to a quick bite to eat and charm you with my deep theoretical analysis on why gingerbread is a subpar cookie to other Christmas cookies."

"Biscuits, West. You're in Scotland now. We call them biscuits. Now how could a lass such as myself turn down such an enticing offer?" Putting my arm through his, I pushed away thoughts of tomorrow and let myself enjoy the moment as West snuck me out of the back door and away from the chaos of the Book Bitches in the front room.

They could clean up their own mess.

CHAPTER SIX

West

"That'll be twenty quid." A woman named Hilda, who was not to be trifled with, surveyed me over her clipboard, a serious look on her face, as I pulled out my wallet and dug out a twenty-pound note. The air in the pub was somber, and I was beginning to understand just how seriously people took this competition.

"You can select your supplies from the table over there. May the odds favor you and all that." Hilda dismissed me and turned to the next in line.

"Jeez," I whispered to Maisie. "This is far more intense than I was expecting."

"You should be here when the knitting club does competitions."

I winced, imagining being impaled by a knitting needle for saying the wrong yarn-related comment, and followed

Maisie to a long table that had been set up at the side of the pub. There, neat packages held pre-selected ingredients to help build the foundation of your home—or barn—and next to it were a variety of add-ons of your choice. Taking a bowl, I studied some gumdrops carefully before selecting a few colors I preferred, along with some sprinkles, and red-hot candies for décor. I wasn't yet sure what I would build, but most of the fun would come from watching Maisie. Already, she'd completely shut me out, having pulled her curls into a lopsided knot on the top of her head, as she fiercely examined each candy item like a mechanic about to buy a used car.

"Worried they've added some exploding candy?" I whispered into her ear, and she gave me a side-eye.

"I wouldn't put it past them."

"People are going to riot if you don't get a move on, Maisie," Graham said, as he walked past with his arms full of empty glasses. Turning, I saw the line growing behind us and more than one annoyed look being sent in our direction.

"Away and shite, Graham." Maisie smiled sweetly.

"That's a bonnie lass, isn't it? I'd keep my eyes on this one, West. She's likely to bite if provoked."

Maisie bared her teeth at Graham, and I laughed, nudging her shoulder.

"I'm going to find us a table. You can take as long as you like, but I'm new here. I still want people to like me."

"Och, they'll get over it." Maisie waved my words away and I left her to it, finding a table near the bar that had a festive red and green tartan tablecloth. Sitting down, I dug through my bowl and began to sort my items, trying to drum up ideas for what I'd build.

Graham appeared at my side and handed me a napkin.

"What's this for?" I asked.

"Your tears."

"My tears? Why do you say that?" I squinted up at him.

"Have you ever tried to make a gingerbread house before?" The gleam in Graham's eye made me realize that I might be in for more of a challenge than I had anticipated.

"No, I can't say that I've given this competitive sport a try."

"It's okay if you cry. Gingerbread house building is not for the faint of heart," Maisie warned as she sat next to me.

"I'm not going to cry." *Was I going to cry?* I certainly hoped not. From my estimation, women didn't generally fall at the feet of men who cried over decorating mishaps.

"Mark my words. There will be tears this night." Maisie's tone was ominous, and I raised my eyebrows at Graham.

"A pint?" Graham asked.

"Oh yes, and I'll probably be on to whisky before long from the looks of it."

The bell clanged and we all looked up to see Hilda standing by the fireplace. It was then that I noticed the Book Bitches had commandeered a table across the room and were studiously ignoring us. I wondered if they were beginning to feel a touch of chagrin over their actions from today. Cherise turned and saw me looking at her. She smiled and held two fingers together, mimicking a couple making out, her eyebrows raised in question. It was about as subtle as a bulldozer running through a brick wall and I grimaced at her, shaking my head. Her face fell, and she bent to whisper to the other women. Lovely. I'd probably just given them more ammunition to set up another "accidental" romantic moment between Maisie and me. I'd need to call the women off. Their enthusiasm was terrifying and I'd had no idea the ruthless efficiency they'd lend to the task at hand.

"You have three hours. Clock starts now."

"Three hours?" I asked, surprised.

"You'll be lucky to finish in that time. If you can even construct anything at all." Maisie smirked.

"Does my impending failure amuse you?" I quirked a brow at her as I dipped a knife in some icing, having seen a few people at the other tables do so, and began to spread some on a piece of gingerbread.

"I think I'd like to see your feathers ruffled a bit," Maisie said, already building her foundation. She bit her lower lip as she picked up another piece of gingerbread, moving it around the board to test locations for it. "Your confidence is intimidating."

At that, I laughed softly to myself. If she had any idea how hard I'd fought for that confidence.

"Yes, being a professor of literature is nothing, if not, the most manly of jobs to hold. You should see how others cower in fear when I walk into the gym." I pretended to flex a muscle and was rewarded with a smile from Maisie.

"Seriously though," Maisie said, reaching for another piece of gingerbread, while I'd barely slathered two of my pieces with icing. "You have this quiet self-assurance. Like you can handle whatever life throws at you. I admire it. It also makes me want to muck you up a bit."

"If you start throwing frosting, I'm out." Although the idea of licking frosting off Maisie's delectable lips held its own appeal.

"Now that would really start a riot. Och, could you imagine if I interrupted everyone's process right now? Look at them all."

I looked around the largely silent room, the occasional curse word breaking the quiet, and realized that I was deeply in trouble. Most people already had some of their walls up.

"There's Fergus. The sheep farmer." Maisie nodded to where one man, in bib overalls and with a ruddy windswept complexion, was already carefully affixing a roof to his structure with the precision of a brain surgeon. I looked woefully down at my two pieces of slathered gingerbread.

"My confidence is dwindling," I admitted, grabbing another piece of cookie to ice. "Soon I'll be reduced to those awkward teen years where I'll just hide in the corner with my book."

"Rough go of it growing up?" Maisie asked, adding another wall.

I really needed to decide what I was building. Looking around in dismay, I realized I could already see cute cottages and homes taking shape. But we'd never had anything like that near us where I grew up. So instead, I decided to go with what I knew. A little surf shack on the beach should suffice. And, since it was open-air, I could do without all the walls. Pleased with my decision, I tested the icing to see if it would hold the cookie pieces together.

They immediately fell apart, and Maisie snorted.

"To answer your question, yes, I had a rough go of it." I

picked the pieces back up and tested them against each other, annoyance growing that the icing wasn't doing much to work as an adhesive. "Despite my dashing good looks and seductive machismo you see before you now, I was once a gangly awkward teenager with glasses and a propensity to stick my nose in a book. It made me an easy target."

"Bullies?" Maisie asked, her blue eyes sympathetic as she looked up at me. Nodding, I pushed up the sleeve of my sweater to reveal a scar that had faded over time.

"Compound fracture was the worst of it."

"What?" Maisie exclaimed, leaning closer to examine the scar, and her silky hair brushed my cheek. "They did that? Clarty bastards. West, that's *awful*."

"It was awful. That one got the main bully suspended and thrown into juvie. But, I just found it easier to keep my head buried in books."

"Hence the whole literature thing, eh. What's your favorite thing about books?" Maisie asked, smearing some icing on a plate and dusting various sprinkles over it to test colors.

"I wouldn't even know where to begin. As a child, I'd say my favorite thing was that they were the perfect shield. Nobody yelled at you if you were reading a book. It's a socially acceptable way to tune out from the world, to disengage, and I never got in trouble for watching too much television or playing video games for too long. Instead, my parents largely let me be so long as I had a book in my hand. It didn't exactly add to my street cred in school, I guess, but I got used to being a loner."

Maisie reached over and squeezed my hand. Darting a look around to see everyone's heads bent to their houses, I turned her hand and quickly pressed a kiss to her palm. She grabbed it back, like my kiss had burned her skin, but a smile hovered at her lips.

"And now? What's your favorite thing about books?"

"I think my favorite thing is that reading is like a shared trip."

"Like an acid trip?" Maisie furrowed her brow and I laughed.

"I suppose you could say an acid trip. Or any trip. I just think it's wild that one hundred different people could read the same story and all see it differently in their heads. This vision plays out in their mind, spun together from the words a storyteller crafts, and yet, if done well, they'll all walk away feeling similar emotions about the story. It's magic, really, this sharing of a world with another, and I think books just create this community among people that allows you to connect. It's really beautiful."

Maisie was watching me openly now, her work suspended, and for a moment I caught a shimmer of tears in her eyes.

"What a lovely way to describe it. I hope to be able to do that someday." Quickly, Maisie bent her head back to her work, but I caught the telltale sniffle.

"Hey." I leaned close and whispered at her ear. "There's no crying in gingerbread house making."

"Oh bugger off." But she laughed, which had been my intention, and while I wanted to ask more about her book, I didn't want to make her sad.

"Maisie," I said, and she glanced at me.

"What?"

"I can't be certain, but I don't think gingerbread is the best material to make gingerbread houses with."

"Oh, and what would you be making your house with then? Oatcakes?" Agnes had overheard me from the next table, and at her words, the entire pub straightened.

Had I just made a cultural faux pas?

"Did the lad just say that gingerbread isn't the right material for a gingerbread house?" Fergus glared at me from where his barn was already sporting a gumdrop roof.

"I was merely suggesting there might be a better base material," I said, the aforementioned confidence that Maisie had admired waning.

"A better material?" Fergus scoffed as though I'd suggested we use slabs of fish.

"And what would you suggest then?" Esther asked, skewering me with a look.

"While I admit that I'm not the most qualified person to make such judgments, perhaps shortbread?"

The pub took a collective inhale, and I swear I would have run and cowered in a corner if Maisie wasn't sitting there looking gleefully at me.

"Or ... tablet. Your famous dessert! A Scottish treasure that surely would be stronger for building blocks than ... this." I looked woefully down at where my two gingerbread pieces tented together on the table.

"Tablet?" Fergus tapped a finger to his mouth and everyone in the pub paused, waiting on the sheep farmer to be the one to render the ultimate decision on the tenacity of tablet as a foundational material for a baked goods decorative challenge. "Now there's a thought."

I exhaled, hoping that would be the last of it but it seemed I was not to be so lucky.

"But then you'd have to cut the tablet in uniform squares, and make sure each lined up correctly," Shannon protested.

"It's the same as cutting shortbread, is it not?" Meredith argued.

"Get tae—"

"What's your mortar then? Icing as well? Wouldn't the tablet soften in the warmth?" Hilda interrupted Esther's curse. Esther glared at her and mumbled something under her breath.

"Tablet house does not have the same ring to it as gingerbread house does," Maisie said, joining the fray.

"Lovely, let's add fuel to this fire, shall we?" I asked.

"Shortbread house is cute, though," Cherise said, winking at me across the room.

"Shortbread," Fergus scoffed. "If you make it right, it crumbles too easily."

"A wee tablet hoose." Hilda shook her head. "Naw. It doesn't have the same charm."

"You could rename it then, couldn't you? If the tablet builds stronger walls, and is easier to work with, maybe you could give it its own name?" I suggested, and again, the pub gave a collective inhale.

"It's called a gingerbread house for a reason, lad," Fergus told me sternly.

"I understand. But things can be renamed, can't they?"

"What do you suggest, West?" Maisie asked, supremely enjoying my discomfort. I couldn't help myself, and I kicked her under the table. She snorted, her eyes dancing, and I glared at her. Graham appeared at my side with a whisky.

"You'll be needing this, lad."

"What is tablet made of again?" I asked, desperate for an out.

"Sugar, condensed milk, and butter," at least seven different people said at once.

"Sugar house! You could call it sugar house. Or sugarplum house if you were feeling festive." I seized on the ingredients in desperation, but Maisie just shook her head woefully at me.

"Sugarplum house? Made of tablet? Sugarplums aren't even the same thing as tablet. They're round." Fergus eyed me like I was the next of his sheep that needed shearing. It took me a moment to remember that Scottish tablet was similar to fudge.

"But you could make igloos with them, since they're round, right? Christmas igloos," I said, sweat breaking out on my brow.

"Might I suggest you quit now?" Agnes leaned over to me, sliding her finger across her throat in a cutting motion.

"Christmas igloos?" Fergus made a motion as though he was going to stand from the table and the woman sitting next to him put her hand on his shoulder. From the looks of it, I might as well have suggested they use cocaine instead of powdered sugar on their cookies.

"Like ... at the north pole? Igloos? Elves? Santa's helpers?"

"One hour," Hilda announced, saving me from my impending doom, and everyone bent to their houses, though periodically I would hear a derisive comment about shortbread houses.

"This … this is not working," I said, exasperated. No matter what I did, my surf shack was not taking shape. At best, I could lean the rectangles of gingerbread against each other to form a tent of sorts, and at this point, I'd just have to work with it. I grabbed some gumdrops to try and build a palm tree, and at the last second, my tower tumbled apart and rolled across the table.

Maisie hiccupped a laugh, and I caught a gumdrop before it hit the floor.

"Stupid gumdrops. Stupid gingerbread."

"There's the Christmas spirit." Maisie had an actual cottage taking shape in front of her, complete with a standing roof, and neat little red dots framing her front door. How had she managed to cut out a door? I looked at my sad pile of gingerbread and scattered gumdrops.

"Why is yours so nice?"

"I'm naturally talented in everything that I do." Maisie stuck her nose in the air.

"You're cute. Even when you're being deeply annoying."

"I warned you this competition would get intense."

"Stupid competition," I grumbled, sticking my fingers in the icing and trying once more to slap some gingerbread cookies together. "Did you know that gingerbread men cookies don't even have their roots in Christmas?"

This time Maisie's eyes rounded as the pub fell dead silent.

"You're going to get yourself kicked out," Maisie hissed, kicking me under the table.

A chair scraped and I kept my eyes on my gingerbread catastrophe, trepidation building as someone crouched next to me.

"You take that back," Fergus said, his eyes level with mine.

"Historically speaking…" I trailed off as Fergus's hands clenched and his ruddy face flushed even more red if that was even possible.

"My apologies," I said smoothly. "It appears I've been misinformed."

"You have." Fergus eyed the mess in front of me. "Let the icing set for a few minutes before you put the walls together. It helps."

"Thanks for the tip."

Fergus stood and ambled back to his table, and Graham took the opportunity to turn the Christmas music up in the background. I nodded my thanks to him.

"Nae bother, lad. I'd rather not clean up blood over a decorating challenge."

"It wouldn't be the first time," Agnes said.

"Och, it was one time, Agnes. I didn't fight back, did I then?"

"Because the lad was double your size." Agnes smiled. "I'm not one for violence, but you shouldn't have been making time with his woman."

"His woman told me she was single. How was I to know?"

"Where does baked goods play into this?" Maisie asked.

Graham sighed and pinched his nose.

"The Christmas cookie bake-off of 2019. Graham had entered the contest with a new recipe. A recipe that apparently, only one other woman knew. One of the judges was her boyfriend."

"You bake?" I turned to Graham. He shrugged one shoulder, and then gave Agnes a slow smile.

"If I have the right incentive. And trust me, she was very willing to share her ... recipes with me."

"Och, Graham, you deserved that bloody nose, I'll tell you that much. I've a mind to bloody it just now myself." Agnes brandished her fist.

"Thirty minutes," Hilda warned, and then there was no more talking.

When the bell clanged, sounding the end of the competition, I looked hopelessly down at the mess in front of me. At best, it looked like a surf shack after a tropical storm had blown through. Maisie's looked like a cute cottage from a Christmas fairy tale, as did many of the houses on the surrounding tables.

For about half a second, I felt the urge to cry.

"I get it now." I turned to Maisie. "No wonder people cry. This is a deeply frustrating sport and I, for one, am willing to admit defeat."

"At least you kept things entertaining." Maisie smiled, leaning over to pat my arm in sympathy. "We were dangerously close to a brawl there for a moment."

"Who knew decorating gingerbread houses could be so contentious?"

"We all do, lad," Fergus called, and I shut my mouth, while the whole pub laughed.

Standing, I took a bow. "I'd like to apologize for my lack of understanding."

"Tablet house." Hilda shook her head in disgust.

Suitably shamed, I sat.

Even though I truly felt ashamed of my efforts, I was also smiling on the inside. *This had been fun.* No, not my lack of creativity ... and nearly being neutered by an aging farmer ... but the friendly banter. This group of people didn't merely tolerate each other. They *welcomed* each other into every facet of their lives. It also clarified how lacking my current life was. I had friends, *tactile* roommates, but not this.

I'd never felt this.

It was a sense of community that shoved my current situation back home into stark relief, shining a light through the cracks in my carefully constructed reality, and for a moment, I realized how desperately lonely I really was. But, maybe, just maybe, life didn't have to be that way.

CHAPTER SEVEN

Maisie

After two days of working on the festival preparations with West, I was ready to explode with need. The man was fulfilling all my Clark Kent buttoned-up fantasies, with his neat glasses, crisp tones, and wide knowledge of books.

Until he kissed me that is.

Then he was all heat and pounding desire and I felt like my soul left my body. All I wanted to do to him were things that would immediately land me on Santa's naughty list. I'd gone from moving freely about my daily life to wondering when I would next see one Weston Smith, aka Professor Dreamy, as some of the book festival volunteers had taken to calling him. Oh yeah, West had a veritable fan club now, and I had to pretend I wasn't the head of it.

Why? Why did I have to pretend I wasn't interested in him? Oh, well, a million reasons I suppose. Mainly though, men like him didn't go for women like me. He was polished, highly educated, and world traveled. I was a small-town girl with big dreams. And damn it, I hated that my insecurities were not letting me be my usual somewhat confident self.

Ever since that kiss ... well, it was the kiss to end all kisses. I swear I just about levitated off the floor that day in the back room of the bookshop. I still got tingles when I thought about it now. On the bright side, I hadn't heard any gossip that he'd been kissing anyone else, or I'd be gutted.

"Are you ready yet?" Agnes called. There was a bite to her tone, and I sighed. She'd been on edge all week with trying to make sure the book festival was perfect. Loren Brae had been battling a bad reputation about being cursed by Kelpies of all things, and everyone in town was doing their best to encourage tourism. And as much as I wanted to pretend the Kelpies weren't real, there'd just been too many eyewitness accounts for me to ignore them. Maybe they didn't like the winter weather, for the town had been quiet since I'd arrived, and I hadn't once been privy to this otherworldly shrieking these Kelpies supposedly did. Either way, I knew Agnes was working hard to reverse whatever curse had brought the Kelpies to Loren Brae and was determined that the festival would be a success for everyone.

It was a lot to unpack, if I was being honest with myself, which is why I often danced around the conversation with Agnes. Or perhaps it was just one of those things that you become accustomed to and just crack on with your daily life —like when you see footage of people collecting flowers in war zones. Life carried on and all that. *Maybe I needed to be a better cousin.* I made a mental note to talk more in depth with Agnes about the Kelpies and see what I could do to help her.

This was the fifth time I'd changed. We'd been invited for dinner at Grasshopper, the new restaurant at MacAlpine Castle, and West would be there along with his best friend, Matthew, who had arrived in Scotland late last night. I hadn't eaten at Grasshopper yet, as it was a touch too dear for my purse, and nerves kicked up as I surveyed my outfit choices.

"What's the holdup?" Agnes asked from my doorway.

"How fancy is the restaurant again? Honestly, I'm just not sure what to wear. I don't want to look …" I lifted my hands and dropped them. Understanding immediately replaced annoyance on Agnes's face and she crossed to examine the choices I'd laid out on her guest bed.

"It's certainly nicer than the pub, but it's not so posh that you couldn't get away with a nice pair of jeans. Let's see here…" Agnes picked up a pair of dark jeans and handed them to me. "Put those on. I have a top for you."

Pulling on the dark jeans, I turned as Agnes came into the room with a midnight-blue silky blouse in her hands.

"This is pretty."

"Try it. I bet the blue tones will make your eyes pop."

Taking the shirt, I slid it over my head, loving how the silk slipped across my skin. It felt sexy, and adult, and … worldly, I supposed. Once I had it on, I turned to the mirror and laughed in delight.

"Agnes! This is a *very* sexy top. It's like, all demure and covered up, but the way the silk drapes …"

"It looks really good on you, Maisie. You should keep it."

"I couldn't."

"I insist. I haven't worn it yet. We'll call it a Christmas gift."

"I mean …" I turned and twirled in the mirror, fluffing out my curls and enjoying the way the silk rippled over my curves. "I won't say no. This is a seriously sexy blouse."

"Shoes?"

"Boots?" I pointed to a pair of black Chelsea boots I had brought with me.

"Those will do. Spruce it up with some jewelry, a touch of lipstick, and we're good to go."

She wasn't wrong, I decided, after I'd followed her orders and checked myself out in the mirror. I didn't need a lot of makeup to make this look pop. For the first time in quite a while, I really cared about how I looked. I suppose I'd gotten in a bit of a rut in that department, as was the nature of small-town life. I mostly saw the same people over and over, and I pretty much had a basic uniform that I wore day-to-day. Jeans, trainers, and a jumper. Easy enough, and it suited me just fine. Perhaps it was a bit ridiculous that a simple top was making me think this deeply about life. Clearly, I needed to shake things up a bit.

"How do I look?" I popped into the lounge with my arms spread and Agnes beamed at me.

"Brilliant, Maisie."

"I feel it, too. Thanks."

Agnes narrowed her eyes at me, and I blanched under her knowing look.

"Is there any *other* reason why you're keen on doing yourself up?"

Busted.

"Och, it's just ... well ...West and I ..."

"West and you?" Agnes closed the front door she'd been about to walk out and stalked over to me, grabbing my shoulders. "There's a West and you and you didn't say something?"

"We've been so busy ..." I trailed off at her furious look. "In fairness, I'm not rightly sure what we are. If there's—"

"Speak. Now." Agnes pointed a finger at me.

"We've kissed twice, and he's asked to court me." At that, I rolled my eyes on a laugh. "Can you believe that? Court me?"

"You've kissed twice?" Agnes's voice rose on a squeak. "When? Where? How did I not know this?"

"Um, the standing stones and in your bookshop."

"In the shop?"

I was fairly certain Agnes was going to have a fit soon, so I made a great show of checking the time.

"We'd better go."

"I'm not done discussing this." Agnes grabbed our coats. "And what has he done to court you? Is that even a thing?"

"I have no idea. But so far, he's been ..." My cheeks pinkened as my heart did a funny shiver in my chest. "He's been writing me little love notes. And poetry. And drawings. And leaving them wherever I am. He slips little notes in my bag. On top of my coffee. In my mittens. Just stuff like that."

"Just stuff like that?" Agnes almost screeched. "That's like, *the* most romantic thing."

I pulled my coat on and shoved my hands in the pocket to feel the telltale crinkle of paper in one of the pockets.

Pulling it out, I pressed my lips together as my whole body warmed.

"Is that one? Let me see."

Agnes peered over my shoulder as I opened it.

On the paper was a small sketch of a dinosaur. Under it was written: *You have me raptor around your finger.*

I snorted.

"Stop it. This is like, seriously too cute," Agnes gushed. I went to shove the paper back in my pocket and she stopped me. "No, you need to be saving these. Are you saving them?"

"I am," I admitted. "I put them in my journal each night."

"Go put it in there before you lose it, and then we have to leave."

On the walk over, Agnes peppered me with questions, and I did the best I could to answer her. It hadn't even been a week since West had arrived, and yet it felt like so much more time had passed. Every day he made it a point to find me and work alongside me. Slowly, he was getting me to open up about my book, and life in Scotland, all while I showered him with questions about sunny California. It seemed like such a world away from what I knew, and I was growing to enjoy our talks about his life as a professor. It must be where he got his easy confidence from, having to stand in front of a lecture hall, and I admired the courage it took to speak to large groups every day.

"What's Matthew like?" I asked Agnes as we walked through the gates of MacAlpine Castle. The night was clear, though cold, and the wind held the promise of snow.

I certainly hoped so, as I wanted my sleigh ride, but I'd just be happy for something different than freezing rain.

"Matthew is wonderful. He's an archeology professor. Whip-smart, extremely kind, and very funny. We all missed him when he had to return to the States. I know Sophie has been doing her best to drag him back to Loren Brae."

"I haven't seen Sophie in a while." Sophie had inherited MacAlpine Castle from her uncle Arthur and had subsequently moved here and fallen in love with Lachlan, one of the managers of the castle. She was delightfully American, a cheerful and confident woman, and I always enjoyed my time with her when I did get to see her. She'd been sick with a cold, which was why I'd missed her at quiz night, and now I looked forward to catching up with her.

We followed the paved road that wound between a line of tall hedges and up a hill until an impressive castle popped into view, like a beautiful woman coming out of a dressing room. Agnes let out a low whistle.

"Archie's gone all out this year."

Did I say like a beautiful woman coming out of a dressing room? Let's amend that thought to a beautiful woman wearing sequins head to toe and coated in diamonds.

"Wow, she certainly sparkles, doesn't she?" I laughed.

"Look! A sleigh!" Agnes pointed to where a sleigh had been pulled in front of the castle and decorated with pretty tartan bows.

There had to be thousands of Christmas lights. I didn't envy the person who had been tasked with putting them up, but it had been well worth the effort. White twinkling lights lined the parapet and circled the four towers, and the doors and windows were all framed in lights. The trees and the gardens behind were coated with strands of lights in soft hues of red, green, and gold. The entire place shimmered and danced, as though the castle itself had come alive. It was time for it to shine.

Suddenly, I felt a funny tug at the back of my neck like someone was watching me. Turning, I glanced over my shoulder at where the dark waters of Loch Mirren reflected the lights of Loren Brae. A ripple drifted across the surface, and a shiver trickled down my spine. Maybe the tourists weren't wrong, maybe there really were Kelpies here. If I was honest with myself, as a proud Scotswoman, it was hard not to get caught up in our myths and legends on occasion.

Some would say that was the fun part of it all—to believe.

Maybe the Kelpies were like Santa Claus, and they only appeared to those who believed—not that seeing a Kelpie was a good thing. From my understanding, it was enough to send anyone running in fright, if not worse.

"I'm *so* impressed. I don't think I've ever seen it so done up before," Agnes mused, twinkle lights reflecting in her wide eyes. "I bet Sophie had a hand in this. She loves Christmas."

"Is this a private dinner tonight or is the restaurant open?" We walked along the side of the castle toward where the restaurant was situated near the car park. MacAlpine Castle was a proper castle with four wings, two of which were kept historically accurate and offered tours for guests. Private apartments filled the other two wings and that is where Sophie and her boyfriend, Lachlan, lived along with the caretakers, Hilda and Archie. Since Lia, the chef, had opened Grasshopper, the restaurant had been booked up most nights. But now only a few cars were parked in the lot.

"I think just friends tonight. The next few weeks will be mental for Lia, what with everyone coming to town for the festival tomorrow, so this is kind of an early Christmas dinner for friends and family."

"Is it? She'll open on Christmas?" I asked, surprised. Most restaurants closed.

"She is. Lia told me she'd learned that a lot of people are quite lonely on Christmas or don't have the energy to cook a big meal. She said she's booked up."

"I suppose that makes sense." As someone who rarely cooked for herself, I could get behind that sentiment.

A sharp bark was the only warning I had before two fuzzballs raced down the path and challenged us.

"Well, Sir Buster, aren't you looking dapper in your kilt tonight? And Lady Lola, looking lovely as well." Agnes smiled at the vibrating chihuahua who wore a little tartan vest and kilt and bared his teeth at us in a low growl. The other dog, a corgi mix of sorts, wore a massive tartan bow and smiled up at us, her chunky bum wiggling in delight.

"What a pair these two are." I laughed. "Grumpy sunshine in dog form."

Sir Buster growled at me in agreement. I bent to pet Lola, not wanting to risk my fingers with Sir Buster, and only when he got annoyed with Lola getting more attention did he sidle closer to me until finally, he'd worked himself under my hand. I took that to mean he wanted all of the scratchies and gave him a proper rub down, before he took off to assault the next guest. Lady Lola followed at a more leisurely pace, seemingly pleased with the world.

"Good evening, ladies."

That sexy polite tone sent a dance of awareness across my skin, and I turned to see West in a suitcoat and jeans, carrying Sir Buster. That traitor.

"I can't believe he let you pick him up," Agnes said to West. "You must have a way with animals."

You can have your way with me too. And why was I jealous of a dog all of a sudden? *That would be because you know what it's like to be in West's arms.*

Right. Not exactly the thoughts I needed to be having when going into a friendly Christmas dinner, but it was hard not to drool over this man in his buttoned-up shirt and coat, glasses, and was that ... yes, a hanky. Never in my life had I given much consideration to a hanky being sexy before, but suddenly I wanted to pull it out of his coat pocket and wave the flag of surrender. West had already told me he was leaving the first week of January, so maybe I *should* just have a holiday fling. A wee Christmas present to myself, I guess. We might be worlds apart when it came to a real-life relationship, but did that really matter when it came to just having some fun? Friends with benefits? A wee cuddle on a cold winter's night?

"Maisie?" Agnes said and I blinked at her, realizing that I'd just been openly staring at West in silence while he smiled at me. His grin widened when I flushed, caught by Agnes, and I turned to stalk toward the door of the restaurant.

"It's too cold to be standing out here," I said over my shoulder as way of explanation for my beeline into the restaurant. Once inside, I took a few deep breaths as I hung up my coat. *Steady, girl. You've got this.*

"What a lovely—"

Turning, I tripped over the leg of the coatrack and went flying forward.

Directly into West's arms. Well, arm that is. The other still held an enraged Sir Buster who barked at me as West caught me close. Agnes managed to stop the coat stand from toppling over.

"Shit," I said, embarrassment creeping through me. Could I stick out any more in the nice restaurant? If this was any indication how my evening was going to go, it might be best if I just leave now.

"Don't worry, darling. I did the exact same thing when I came in." I turned at a cheerful American voice. An older woman in sequin pants, a screaming hot-pink sweater, and a sparkly fascinator on her head walked toward me with her arms open. West released me and the woman drew me into a quick hug. Surprised, I let her, though we'd never met.

"I didn't really, but I don't want you to feel embarrassed in front of your young man," the woman whispered in my ear and then pulled back. "I'm Lottie, by the way, Sophie's honorary mother."

"Oh! So nice to meet you. I'm Maisie, and this is my friend, Weston." I emphasized the word friend while Lottie shook West's hand and then gave Agnes a long hug.

"Lottie! When did you arrive? Oh, I'm so delighted you're here."

"Me too," Lottie gushed, slapping a hand on her sequined pants. "I flew in with Matthew as we couldn't bear to be away from Sophie a moment longer. Plus, it's nice to have a properly cold Christmas, isn't it? The weather just doesn't want to cooperate for my mood in California."

Immediately, I liked this woman, a gentle mix of motherly and eccentric, and I knew she'd be my safe harbor if I felt uncomfortable at all this evening.

"I don't know. I think I'd take some of your California sunshine if I could," Agnes argued as another man approached. He was smartly dressed in dark pants, a tartan jacket, and a Lady Gaga T-shirt. Clamping a hand on West's shoulder, he beamed at us.

"Hi, friends."

"There he is," West exclaimed, turning to give who I assumed was Matthew an awkward half-armed man hug while Sir Buster increased his growling until he sounded like a motorcycle revving its engine.

"I'm just going to put this ticking time bomb down," West said, and gingerly placed the dog on the floor.

"Smart move, brother. It's a toss-up if he wants to kill you or kiss you."

"How was the flight?" West asked.

"Smooth as possible. Plus, traveling with Lottie is a joy."

Lottie preened next to me and then leaned in for a stage whisper.

"Matthew just likes using the private jet."

"I mean, someone has to use it, no? It's horribly uneconomical to have that just sitting around if you're not flying often. I'm just justifying your expense, Lottie."

My eyes rounded. A private plane? I was so out of my league.

"And who is this lovely lady?" Matthew turned to me.

"This is Maisie," West said. But he didn't say it … casually. It was all, *this* is Maisie. With an undertone. A meaning. Something more there. When Matthew's eyes flew to mine and his grin widened, I realized that West had been talking to his friend about me.

"*Delighted* to meet you," Matthew said, taking my hand and kissing it lavishly.

A flash of light ... or movement ... or something breezed through the air, and I jolted as something touched my head.

"What the—" West looked around, his hands in the air, and my mouth fell open.

On his head was a headband with reindeer horns.

A giggle worked its way up my throat.

"Oh dear." Agnes sighed. I blinked at her. She now wore a headband with a Christmas tree sticking up from it.

"Did that just—" Matthew looked around. He had a Santa cap on his head. Gingerly I reached up and found I, too, now wore a headband.

"What's mine?" I asked weakly, unsure what had just happened.

"Candy cane," West informed me, his eyes darting around the room.

"Seriously, what just happened?" I gasped, torn between laughter and fear. I noted Lottie still just wore her fascinator.

Agnes looked to Matthew and nodded toward West.

"Is he cool?"

"He's cool," Matthew assured her.

"I'm also standing right here," West pointed out mildly.

"Right ... so," Agnes started and then pressed her lips together.

"Best to just rip the Band-Aid off." Matthew laughed.

"Well, then. In a nutshell? The castle is haunted, magick

is real here, and Lia, the chef, has a broonie named Brice. A kitchen elf if you will. Most people don't know about him, so we like to keep him a secret."

"Oh wheesht." I lightly smacked Agnes's arm and threw my head back and laughed. "Surely she's just having you on, West."

"I'm not."

"It's all real, dear. The Kelpies, the magickal Order of Caledonia, the broonie. Isn't that fabulous? Aside from the murderous Kelpies, of course." Lottie and Agnes exchanged a knowing look. "But what a life we get to live knowing that magic is real."

"We did see a ghost coo the other night," West put in and my eyes met his. A small smile passed between the two of us and I caught Matthew watching.

"You met Clyde?" Lottie beamed. "I have yet to meet this infamous Clyde, but I can't wait. He sounds like he's great fun."

"Clyde?" West and I said at the same time. I laughed. *Of course,* the ghost coo would have a name.

"Yes, he fancies himself quite the prankster," Agnes said.

A whoosh of air breezed past and I swore I caught a blur of movement before a cocktail appeared in my hand. I gripped it tightly before I dropped it and gaped down at the champagne glass.

"Did anyone—" I looked up to see everyone else now holding champagne glasses. Agnes pinched her nose with her free hand.

"So, Lia's said it's become a wee bit of a problem just in the last week or so since a friend visited who has a younger child. I guess they were talking about Elf on the Shelf, and Brice overheard it and was so taken with the concept that he's really, well, he's escalated, let's just say."

"Escalated?" West raised an eyebrow. Kelpies were one thing. But were we seriously talking about a magickal kitchen elf? It seemed Agnes had been holding out on me when it came to the magickal beings inhabiting Loren Brae. I couldn't decide if I was relieved or annoyed that I'd been kept in the dark. Magick, in any manner, could be largely disconcerting when you first experienced it. I was still reeling from the run-in with the ghost coo the other night, and now I needed to recalibrate my understanding of the world around kitchen elves.

That being said, my inner ten-year-old, who lived for fairy tales, was kind of dying a bit from excitement.

"I think *he* thinks he's being helpful. But, as we know from people who lock themselves in the back room of bookstores together, *helpful* can be open to interpretation."

Should I murder my cousin? Maybe I could get the broonie to do it.

"In all fairness, we completed the task given to us and the books were delivered to their assigned places with zero margin of error," West said. How could he talk like this when she was referencing the kiss to end all kisses? My cheeks flamed and I buried my face in my champagne glass.

"My, my, my," Matthew intoned and threaded his arm through mine. "I do believe my night just got a lot more interesting. Come, Maisie, and let me tell you all the embarrassing things I know about Weston."

"Oh, please do," I said, breathing a sigh of relief as

Matthew dragged me away from the group and toward the restaurant. "Thank you."

"You looked like you needed a break there, sweetie. Now, what do you want to know more? Embarrassing facts or West's dating history?"

I shouldn't ask about any of this, I lectured myself, before curiosity won out.

"Dating," I whispered, and Matthew beamed.

"I would have chosen the same myself. So, he's one of my best friends and I won't give too many details as that's for him to tell you. But he's ... careful in who he chooses to date."

"Careful?" I raised an eyebrow.

"Yes, he's not one for wild nights or random one-night stands. He doesn't date employees, nor will he touch any of the various undergrads that show up to flirt at his office. He's a man of honor, guarded, and doesn't give his heart easily."

"He's been hurt," I guessed.

Matthew angled his head.

"He has, but it's been a while. Long enough now that I was starting to worry that he'd given up on women entirely. Until he told me he'd met someone."

"I'm not ..." Panic skittered through me at his words. This sounded way more serious than the holiday fling that I had just given myself permission to enjoy.

"You *are*." Matthew regarded me with a serious look. "You very much are someone, Maisie."

Taking a sip of my champagne, I let the effervescent liquid cool my throat, as worry slipped through me.

Mistletoe appeared mid-air, hovering wildly in front of

my face, as though held by nothing, and I almost dropped my champagne. The leaves shook angrily at me, as though I was purposely ignoring them, instead of being in shock.

"Wrong pairing, Brice. She's not mine."

A disgruntled muttering came from mid-air and the mistletoe vanished.

"I'm going to need another drink," I decided.

When one appeared in my hand with a gentle nudge, all I could do was laugh.

Ghost coos, Kelpies, and broonies ... and sexy men who have mentioned me to their best friends. What a night.

CHAPTER EIGHT

Maisie

"And then ... then he ..." Lia was laughing so hard she had tears running down her face. "...threw whipped cream into Munroe's parents' faces."

The group of us drinking whisky in the lounge laughed. Lia and her fiancé, Munroe, snuggled by the fire, her sitting on the floor and leaning back between his legs, while Sophie and Lachlan cuddled into each other on the sofa. Archie and Hilda, the castle caretakers, sat in matching loungers, and Lottie, Matthew, West, Agnes, and I were all divided between another couch and the floor. On a coffee table in front of us lay a game that Munroe had insisted wasn't a very involved board game like he preferred, so we'd all agreed to play a round.

"Och, the lad's been a touch tricky lately. He hid my car keys the other day so I wouldn't leave," Munroe said.

"Honestly, it's the Elf on the Shelf thing. He's taken his own interpretation of it and gone wild. The other day I came into the kitchen to find every utensil I owned gone. Just gone. It wasn't until I had an absolute fit that he returned them." Lia rolled her eyes.

"Cheeky lad." Lachlan laughed.

"Just so long as it doesn't mess up any dinner service." Lia furrowed her brow and tucked a strand of loose hair behind her ear. "I don't want anyone to have a bad Christmas."

"Is this his first Christmas with you?" I asked, surprised that I was speaking so casually about a magickal wee broonie who lived in the shadows of the kitchen. But nevertheless, here we were. Maybe it was the whisky making me much more accepting of this whole magick thing.

"It is, yes." Lia looked to me.

"Perhaps the wee lad is just acting out a bit. Hoping you'll have a gift for him. Or even, you know, keep him around. Sounds like he doesn't have much in the way of family."

"That's ... that's entirely possible." Lia looked to Munroe, her heart in her eyes, and he squeezed her shoulder.

"We'll make sure he knows he's loved," Munroe assured her.

A happy tinkling of bells sounded from somewhere in the castle and Lia nodded.

"I think you're right, Maisie. That was one of his happy sounds."

"Brice with bells on." Lachlan laughed. The bells chimed more loudly, and we all laughed. I couldn't believe how easily West seemed to be taking this all in. I'd grown up with a lot of these myths and legends, and though it wasn't every day that I ran across a broonie, I'd certainly heard enough stories over the years to not run screaming from the castle either. But West? He seemed to be cool as a cucumber. I wondered what it would take to see him rattled, and a part of me realized that I wanted to mess him up a bit, ruffle his feathers so to speak.

"Whatever has that look in your eye, I suggest you redirect your thoughts before I throw you over my shoulder and drag you to a dark tower in this castle and explore your ideas further."

My mouth dropped open as I realized that I'd been openly ogling West and he'd, correctly, interpreted the direction of my thoughts. Snapping my gaze away, I tapped a finger on the table.

"Are we going to play?" Was I ignoring his comment? Absolutely. Was the fire of a thousand suns basically burning inside me needing his hands on my body? Also, yes.

"Yes, let's!" Sophie clapped her hands. "I made Matthew bring it for me for Christmas. It's too much fun. Basically, you all pull a card with a phrase on it. Then you have to draw it. Pass your board to the person on the right, and they will write what they think you drew. Then the next person has to draw what the person before thought it was. It goes all the way down the line until it returns to you. Then you lay the cards out and see if people were able to match your beginning description. Kind of like Telephone, but with drawing. Just a warning, the cards are a bit naughty too."

"Just like my girl," Lachlan muttered into Sophie's neck and then nibbled her ear. Her skin flushed, and I pretended to not have overheard the comment. Was it hot in here? I shouldn't be this warm in just a silk blouse in the middle of a Scottish winter.

We all drew cards and I let out a tiny sigh of relief at the description.

A Christmas Palm Tree.

Easy enough. And it shouldn't be too hard to draw, not that I was particularly well-inclined in that area. I bent my head to the task, carefully drawing the long trunk, the rounded roots at the bottom, and the leaves shooting from the top. Then, I dotted the trunk with lights, wishing I had colored markers to work with. Once I was certain I had a winning drawing, I capped my marker and handed it off to West who immediately gave me a wide-eyed look.

"What?" I demanded, ready to defend my work.

"No table talk," Sophie ordered.

West winked at me, and I narrowed my eyes, suspicious of what he was thinking. But just then Lottie handed me her drawing and I gaped down at it.

"Is that—" I began, horrified, and Sophie hissed at me.

"Sorry, sorry, sorry." I swallowed a giggle at the drawing of a buff man in teeny-tiny Speedos, very artfully done, mind you, with a lot of attention to detail, and then bananas relaxing in a hammock. Hoping I was interpreting the drawing correctly, I wrote down my guess and passed it on. The game went quickly, with a lot of muffled snorts and outright laughter, as everyone tried to figure out what each drawing meant. By the time my cards had returned to me, the evening had taken on that warm glow of relaxation and joy that came with hanging with good people around a warm fire on a cold winter's night.

They started on the other side of the table, with Matthew.

"This is preposterous," Matthew said, stabbing a finger at the cards. "I don't know how a zombie going to the dentist turned into the headless horseman, but you all clearly need better interpretation skills."

"Ohhhh," Lachlan said, nodding in sudden understanding. "I thought that guy was cutting the zombie's head off."

"No. He was clearly getting his teeth cleaned. See?" Matthew waved his card in exasperation, and we all laughed. When we reached Lottie, I was delighted to see that my guess had been correct. She laid her cards out in a row, and we all cheered when the term "Banana hammock" made it through to the end. Hers was the first to do so, and my blood heated as it came to my turn. Lottie was sweet and all, but it was time to take the older woman down.

"Well, I'm sure you all guessed mine as well," I said, and then shrieked when I turned the cards over. My mouth dropped open. "Bloody hell ... ejaculation? Glitter dong? Are you guys kidding me?"

"It was pretty clear from the drawings." Matthew shrugged.

Narrowing my eyes, I turned on West.

"*You*. You did this. This is your fault. You knew what I was drawing."

"What was it supposed to be, dear?" Lottie leaned over.

"A Christmas palm tree," I bit out, annoyance making me grumpy.

"Ahhh," West said, nodding now. "That makes more

sense. I was wondering what all the dots over the shaft were."

"The dots over the ..." I slapped my forehead. "*Why* would there be dots?"

"Ants?" Lachlan suggested.

"Chocolate sprinkles?" Lia asked.

"Glitter?" Matthew asked.

"Let's see your drawing, Maisie," Matthew said, and I held it up. The whole group nodded.

"Definitely a sparkle peen," Matthew said, and I threw up my hands.

"You know, dear, I'm quite a good artist. I'm happy to give you drawing lessons," Lottie offered.

"I don't need ... this is a *great* drawing of a Christmas palm tree," I insisted and took in everyone's skeptical looks.

"You really are competitive, aren't you?" West smiled at me, and I flushed under his knowing look.

"It's not, I just, okay, *yes*, I like to win," I admitted, taking a small sip of my whisky. Was there anything wrong with that? Didn't most people like to win?

"It's cute," West said, and I furrowed my brow at him. He laughed, and my insides twisted. He looked so right, sitting here among my friends, and I realized that I didn't want him to leave. Not yet. I wanted more time with this man. While I couldn't say what that looked like, I wanted to see if there really was something between us. Or maybe that was just the warm glow of the evening speaking, with most people coupled up, and perhaps I was just feeling wistful. *Perhaps even a touch melancholy that another one of my dreams—being in a relationship—was still unrealized.* Typically, I didn't much think about being single or dating, except there was something about Christmas that seemed to make everyone feel like they had to be in a couple to be happy. For me, I'd often found other ways to celebrate, like going for a hike or treating myself to a day in Edinburgh or I would join Agnes at The Tipsy Thistle to hang with any other stragglers. Honestly, those were the most fun Christmases for me—sitting at the pub and playing games—while lonely people wandered in and remembered that a welcome smile was always nearby.

"Cute?" I sniffed. "Champions aren't cute, West."

"I beg to differ. Buddy Holly, the dog that won at Westminster Dog Show this year, was pretty dang cute."

Sir Buster walked over to West and followed my suit, baring his teeth at West.

"But none more handsome than such an esteemed gentleman as yourself, good sir," West hastily assured him. Sir Buster, seemingly acknowledging the compliment, pawed at West's leg and growled. West looked up in fear.

"Do I dare pick him up? He really gives mixed messages."

"Give it a go, lad. See how you get on," Lachlan said.

"This is more terrifying than the time the undergrad showed up at my office in just a trench coat." West mimicked wiping sweat off his brow and reached for the dog. Ever so gently, he picked up Sir Buster who immediately began to growl. West halted with the dog mid-air, as his growling intensified to high-level rage, and looked up in panic. "What do I do? I don't know what this means."

"He's just a grumpy sort. Tuck him on your lap and he'll settle in," Hilda advised from her chair by the fire.

The growling continued until West had him situated on

his lap, where Sir Buster promptly curled into a ball and snuggled in. A look of relief passed over West's face.

"I thought I was going to lose a finger there for a moment."

"I believe I speak for all of us here"—Lachlan looked around—"but we'd dearly love to hear the trench coat story."

"Yes, West, do tell." I tilted my head. Were his cheeks turning pink?

"Oh God." West buried his face in his hands. "It was my first year as a professor and I had a meeting with the dean in my office. But just before the dean arrived, one of my students stopped by, unannounced. She'd been struggling in class and wanted to ask for extra tutoring."

"I bet she did," I said. I couldn't even fathom having a professor as good-looking as West when I'd been at uni. I doubt I would have concentrated in any lectures, although I wouldn't have been bold enough to approach him. *Just how many women have approached West during his years as a professor?* As soon as I thought that, I recalled Matthew's words about West.

"He's not one for wild nights or random one-night stands. He doesn't date employees, nor will he touch any of the various undergrads that show up to flirt at his office. He's a man of honor, guarded, and doesn't give his heart easily." From what I knew of West, I could now see that.

West slid me a look before continuing.

"I sort of got her meaning when she sat on the corner of the desk and leaned over to stroke her hand down my chest. It was, honestly, terrifying. It had taken me ages to finally land this dream job at this university and the last thing I wanted was any sort of misconduct on my record."

"What did you do?" Munroe asked. West bent to reach for his whisky but the growl from his lap stopped him. Taking pity, I reached down and handed him his glass so he could take a healthy sip.

"I stood up and backed away, luckily. But she also stood and opened her trench coat. Thank God she wasn't fully naked, but the dean walked in just in time for both of us to be treated to a matching lace panty set."

"What color?" Lachlan asked and Sophie elbowed him in the ribs.

"What? You've got me loving lace now," Lachlan grumbled, and Sophie chuckled as he nuzzled into her neck once more.

"I think the dean could see by the look on my face that I hadn't invited her, um, advances and she fled from the office. Needless to say, we still had a long chat about acceptable conduct, and I had to reassure him, several times over, that I wasn't interested in mixing business with pleasure. While it's not technically illegal, it's certainly frowned upon."

"I bet you have a front row full of cute undergrads, don't you?" Lia mused.

"I …" West blushed, and I poked his ribs.

"Are you the hot professor?"

"Ahem." Matthew cleared his throat, putting on an offended air. "Let's not forget the other dashing professor in this room."

"Of course, how could we?" Sophie laughed and turned to us. "Matthew has single-handedly managed to increase enrollment of male students in the archeology program, which, unfortunately is already a male-dominated field."

"Much to my chagrin, as you well know I'm a feminist." Matthew sighed.

"It's not your fault that you're Hottie McProfessor and this one's Dr. Sexy Storybooks."

"Dr. Sexy Storybooks?" I exclaimed, clapping a hand over my mouth.

"I do have a Ph.D."

"As do I. But for some reason he gets the doctor title." Matthew sniffed.

"Do you write sexy stories?" Munroe asked.

"No … it's just … I teach literature, and obviously, there are a lot of romantic stories woven through historical texts. Love is an enduring and popular theme, which is why romance novels continue to dominate the bestseller charts today. In fact, romance is the number one selling genre in the world."

"That makes my heart happy." Sophie sighed.

"I'm surprised you aren't just teaching highbrow literary novels," I said.

"The two aren't mutually exclusive," West said. "Plenty of literary greats also have romantic themes. The Brontë sisters are one such example of authors that embody this."

"Speaking of books," Agnes said, slapping her knees and standing up. "I have to get on. We've an early start with the festival tomorrow and I'm sure I still have a million things to do. Thank you, Lia, for hosting us. It was such a lovely wee gathering for our found family."

I rose, knowing that I needed to be rested for the morning as well.

"I'll second that," I said, smiling my thanks at Lia. "Best meal I've had in ages. The broonie was a fun addition."

Tinkling bells sounded once more, and we all laughed. Everyone seemed to take our departure as cue to leave and West followed us outside.

Glancing at the sky coated in murky grey clouds, West zipped his jacket and joined us as we walked down the lane toward Loren Brae. Wind rippled across the loch, bringing with it the scent of rain, and I burrowed more deeply into the scarf I'd wrapped around my neck.

"Where are you staying again, West?" Agnes asked and I was glad my scarf hid my blush because I, too, was wondering the same thing. And if it was close enough for me to drop in.

"Now that I've figured out where I am, it's about a twenty-minute walk along the road that hugs Loch Mirren." West gestured to the road that ran the other way from Loren Brae. Damn it. I guess a quick night cap with him wouldn't be in the cards. Which was fine. I had other things to be worrying about like making sure this book festival would go off without a hitch.

"Ah yes, the Ferguson cottage. It's a nice wee spot, isn't it?"

A sharp burst of wind shook us, and I caught West shiver out of the corner of my eye.

"It smells like snow, doesn't it?" Agnes wondered, tilting her head up to the sky. "You know that kind of bite the air gets ... almost metallic? It's different than the smell of rain on the wind, isn't it?"

"Sharper," I agreed. "How are you handling the cold, California?"

"I ... it's an adjustment," West conceded with a laugh. We'd reached the bottom of the hill that led from the castle and West turned right with us toward town instead of in the direction of his cottage.

"Are you going to the pub then?" Agnes asked.

"No, I'm walking you two ladies safely home."

"Well, aren't you just the sweetest?" Agnes trilled and a happy bubble worked itself up my throat. Not that I'd invite West in when I was sharing a flat with Agnes, but it was just nice to have someone who cared enough to do something sweet like this. *It's just his manners. Don't get ahead of yourself.*

A flash of light was the only warning we had before Agnes screamed, her hand to her chest, and I found myself, once again, wrapped around West like a barnacle stuck to a ship.

"Damn it, Clyde!" Agnes gasped, her hand at her chest.

The ghost coo was back. This time, he'd decorated his horns with Christmas lights and two unmatched ornaments swung from them like manic earrings. His eyes fell, if that was possible, at Agnes's curse. He trotted a few steps back, his shoulders dropping, and Agnes sighed, pinching her nose.

"Don't worry, Clyde. You look great," West said, holding me tightly. The coo trotted forward, tilting its head so the ornaments swung wildly. "All I want for Christmas is *moo*."

Delighted, Clyde bellowed, shocking us all into almost heart attacks before disappearing.

"Moo-y Christmas?" Agnes asked, weakly, as she patted her heart and gasped for air.

"Santa *Coos* is coming to town?" I couldn't help but add in as I detached myself from West.

"Let it moo, let it moo, let it moo?" West tried and we all groaned.

"You can do better than that," I said.

"Cut me a break, I'm on an adrenaline rush here." West laughed.

"How do you get used to that?" I asked Agnes, still reeling from the fact that not only were ghosts real, but so were broonies. This Christmas holiday was turning out to have quite a few revelations for me. I guess I needed to spend more time in Loren Brae now that I knew the rumors of the hauntings were real. My eyes strayed to the smooth surface of Loch Mirren. I wouldn't be surprised if the Kelpies turned up next. Which, if any stories were to be believed, weren't anything that I had any interest in meeting. Picking up my pace, I bent my head against the icy wind and turned up the street toward Agnes's flat.

"I don't," Agnes said. "It doesn't happen all that often, at least not to me, so it's always a surprise. I think that's what he likes. He made Lia wet her pants a few months ago, a fact that she will not let him forget."

"I don't blame her. I basically climb West every time it happens."

"Every time?" Agnes asked, turning to me. "How many times have you seen him now?"

"Well, just then, of course. And he jumped us the other night at the standing stones. I was a touch close to wetting myself as well."

"Well, would you look at the time?" Agnes slid a look between us and then turned to unlock her door. "That's me

A KILT FOR CHRISTMAS

off to bed then, have a good night you two." Agnes went inside so fast that West barely had a chance to say goodnight before the door shut smartly behind her.

"That's a wee bit obvious—"

West cut off my words with his mouth, pressing me back against the door until the whole world blocked out but the taste of him. His lips were hot on mine, erasing all thoughts from my head except for one.

Him.

I wanted to eat him up like a bottomless pint of ice cream. Desire consumed every inch of my being, and I reached up to run my hands over his chest, gasping as he angled his head and deepened the kiss. Heat licked through my body, the icy wind forgotten, as West's kiss made me forget everything but him. What was it about this man's kisses that made me want to throw caution to the wind? It was like something took over my body, my mind, my soul, and I swear if he asked me to strip naked and jump into the freezing loch—water Kelpies be damned—I'd likely do it.

When he ended the kiss, breaking contact and stepping back, I let out a mewl of distress. Dazed, I looked up at him, wanting, no *needing* more of him.

"I—"

"Say goodnight, Maisie." West smirked.

"But ..." Torn, I didn't know what to do. I wanted this to continue, truly, I did, but I also had commitments to Agnes and no place for this to really continue. West's smile widened.

"I'm going to wait here until you go inside."

"Right, okay. Um, thanks for the ..." I waved my hand

weakly in the air. West laughed and put a hand on my shoulder, gently turning me toward the door.

"Sweet dreams, Maisie."

I held a hand to my mouth the whole way up the stairs, my lips burning from his touch. At the top, Agnes popped her head out of the room and then accosted me when she saw I was alone.

"You didn't invite him up?" Agnes demanded.

"And what? Give you a front-row seat to listen in?" I veered toward my room, ignoring her complaints behind me.

"A girl needs to find her entertainment somewhere."

"Try porn," I suggested over my shoulder before I closed the door to my room.

"As if," Agnes called, and I realized just how smart I'd been not to invite West up. I could hear her as clearly as if she was standing in the room next to me. "Porn is all done through the male gaze. Where's the good stuff for women?"

"Try romance novels."

"Good call, I do have a stack next to my bed."

Laughing, I walked to the window and peeked out of the curtain to just see West walking down the street—a lone man on a cold night—and I wished I had his number to call him and make sure he got home safely. I mean, I knew he would, crime wasn't particularly rampant in Loren Brae, but still my heart hurt watching him walk away like that.

Was it possible to miss someone that I had just met?

Turning, I plopped down on the bed and stared at the ceiling, allowing myself for a brief moment to dream about *what ifs* and *maybes*.

CHAPTER NINE

West

A knock at my door the next morning jolted me awake and I blinked at the ceiling before remembering where I was. Scotland. Reaching over, I swiped my phone to see the time. It was just shy of seven in the morning. Who in the world would be here this early? The festival didn't start until half past ten.

"Yooo-hooo."

"The Book Bitches." I wiped a hand over my face, simultaneously amused and annoyed, and stumbled to the door to let the group of women inside. Today they came carrying shopper bags, and what looked to be a gift as well. They all clambered inside, looking me up and down, and then peering behind me.

"Are you alone?" Meredith asked me. Her sweatshirt today read *Santa Coos is Coming to Town* and sported a drawing of a coo in a Santa hat.

"Yes, I'm alone. Though I suspect this would be quite

daunting for my partner if I was engaged in a romantic tryst, wouldn't it?"

"If she can't handle us then she wouldn't be worth your time," Esther said, unpacking breakfast ingredients on the counter. Her sweater had *Let's get baked* across the front along with a gingerbread man.

"We got you a wee gift," Cherise said, handing me a bag. On her sweatshirt was the phrase *Nice until proven naughty* with candy canes wrapped around each other. I shook my head. Where were these women getting these?

"A gift and breakfast," Shannon amended. She turned from taking her coat off and to my surprise, my cheeks reddened at her shirt. Innocuous spruce trees were centered above the phrase *I like them real thick and sprucy.*

"On you go, take your gift, shower up. We've got ourselves a day ahead of us. We'll just whip up a wee brekkie while you're at it," Esther said, pulling out glasses for orange juice. My stomach grumbled, and I certainly wasn't going to turn down a home-cooked meal, so I retreated to the bedroom clutching the gift bag at my chest. I had to admit, I was more than slightly terrified by what might be in the bag, and I gingerly dipped my hand inside. When I discovered a sweatshirt among the tissue paper, my fear grew.

Drawing the shirt out, I held my breath until I unfolded it, and then laughed.

On it was a highland coo wrapped in Christmas decorations, much like Clyde had been last night. It read: *Chillin' with my Snowmies.* Safe, I breathed a sigh of relief and put it on the bed before hurrying through my morning routine. By the time I was showered and sporting my new Christmas sweatshirt, the scent of bacon and fresh coffee filled the cottage.

A chorus of excitement greeted my arrival as the women gushed over my sweatshirt.

"Thank you for the gift, ladies. I very much appreciate it. Particularly as I can use all the extra layers I can get." Underneath the sweatshirt I had put on a long-sleeved Henley shirt, topped with a flannel button down, and still I feared I wouldn't be warm enough today.

"We needed to debrief with you and organize today's mission." Esther scooped scrambled eggs onto a plate.

"It's important to be tactical." Meredith handed me a cup of coffee.

"We need all of your focus today." Cherise gave me a stern look as I sat at the breakfast bar. Esther slid me a plate heaped with eggs, bacon, toast, and beans and I gaped at the sheer volume of food. That being said, we did have a long day ahead of us, so best I fuel up. Plus, I feared for my life if I didn't clear my plate.

"Ladies," I said, taking a sip of my juice. "Stand down."

"You won her over? See? I knew locking you in a room together would work." Shannon and Esther high-fived.

"I have not won her over. Yet. But we've kissed three times now and I truly feel that I'm starting to win her favor." I bit into a perfectly browned piece of toast and waved it in the air, wondering why I just shared Maisie's and my delicious kisses with these women. I was not in the habit of sharing personal details with *anyone* other than Matthew. And that was only because *nothing* was private with that man. He did not understand boundaries. Something he had in common with the Book Bitches, it seemed. But I didn't believe I needed their help any longer, not after the delicious moment I shared with my dream girl last night. *You need to let these women down gently, West.* "I'm sure I can take it from here."

"Nonsense," Esther huffed, leaning against the counter and crossing her arms over her chest, with the conviction of an army veteran who'd seen it all. "Things can change at any moment. There are too many variables. We'll need to ensure that you land the plane."

I choked on the bite of eggs I'd taken as I imagined the Book Bitches peering in my bedroom window as I seduced Maisie.

"With all due respect, I'd request some privacy in that department." I heaved as Shannon pounded me on the back with her fist.

"The metaphorical plane. Stay with me, lad." Esther snapped her fingers at me, and I nodded dutifully.

"What booth will you be working today?" Cherise asked.

"The ring toss. The books are all wrapped like Christmas gifts and if they get a ring over the top, they can take a book home."

"Perfect, so that's a two-person booth. We'll make sure Maisie is working it as well," Meredith said.

"If she's needed elsewhere—"

"She'll be working it with you." Esther's tone brooked no disagreement.

"Yes, ma'am." I bit back a smile, amused at how these women had so quickly burrowed their way into my life and my personal business. California Weston would find this annoying, but here, I was softening toward the idea of moving away from my solitary lifestyle. It wasn't like I'd chosen the loner lifestyle, either. The loner lifestyle had chosen me at a young age, and I'd run with it. Which is why life with my ex-girlfriend had been so jarring. I'd been forced into so many uncomfortable social situations that when the relationship had ended, I'd run for cover and was just now finally peeking out of my hermit hole.

After breakfast, the ladies hurried me out the door, chattering with excitement for the festival. It was colder today, with icy wind gusts much stronger than the day before, and I pulled my coat more tightly around me, grateful for my new sweatshirt. I hoped the weather would hold off, as the festival was being held mainly in the small open-air square in the center of town. A large tent had been erected, with portable heating lamps tucked in the corners, and booths set up along the edges. Each shop in town had their own book-themed design—the vet's had a display offering books where the dog doesn't die. Silently, I applauded them for that decision.

Downtown Loren Brae was a flurry of activity, with people unloading their trucks and vans, and the coffee cart was doing a brisk business already. The ladies found a parking spot, after numerous arguments, and we got out of the car.

"Thanks for the ride, ladies." I immediately regretted my choice of words when Shannon winked at me.

"Anytime, sailor," Shannon purred.

"Still too young for you," Meredith interjected, grabbing Shannon's arm and pulling her away.

"Don't worry about a thing, dear. We'll get everything sorted." Esther patted my arm and disappeared with

Cherise. I took a breath to steady my nerves, sincerely hoping they didn't *actually* attempt to kidnap Maisie today, and went to find my booth.

Set up in the corner, so there was more room to toss the rings, the booth had just enough room for two people to work behind it, taking tickets, wrapping books, and picking up rings that went rolling. A cardboard Christmas tree was the backdrop and the table tucked to the side had piles of books that still needed wrapping. I bent my head to the task, though I wasn't the most proficient at wrapping gifts, and hummed to myself while the tent filled with people. Outside, the wind gusted, causing the side of the tent to slap against the booth, and I shivered. I'd taken off my coat to show off my new sweatshirt, but I wished the heat lamps did a better job. Scents of cinnamon and nutmeg filled the air, and I made a note to pick up whatever baked yumminess was making the place smell so good. I wouldn't be ready to eat for a long time after that hefty breakfast, but it would be nice for a treat later today.

Voices rose, and I turned in time to see Maisie shoved into my booth.

"She's a bit tetchy today, but she's agreed to help you out," Meredith called.

"I wasn't tetchy until you four bulldozed me." Maisie glared at the women, hands on her hips. I bit back a smile as I watched the stand-off, wondering who would win.

"A bonnie lass as yourself should be working a booth, no? Not stuck in the back of a shop," Cherise said.

Had they dragged her all the way down here from Bonnie Books? My eyes widened.

"I *had* plans to work a booth. The craft book section."

"Craft books? Well, isn't this perfect. Shannon was an art teacher."

I eyed the woman's *thick and sprucy* sweatshirt and wondered if that was where they were coming up with so many different holiday shirts.

"You can't just—"

"Och, it's a driech day, isn't it, love? Why don't we get you a cup of hot cocoa?" With that, all four turned with the precision of a battalion and marched away, leaving Maisie gaping after them with her mouth hanging open.

"Did they just—" Maisie turned to me.

"They're terrifying," I agreed, smiling at her. She looked so pretty today, with her long, dark curls tumbling around her face, a cute red sweater on, and a cozy Santa hat tucked over her head. Her blue eyes narrowed at me and I raised my hands. "Don't look at me like that. I had nothing to do with this."

"Matchmaking old broods," Maisie muttered, and I laughed.

"Come on and help me wrap these gifts. I fear I'm not quite so talented in this department."

Maisie came over to survey my work and I caught a scent of soap and cinnamon. I had to clench my fists to stop myself from reaching out to her for a kiss.

"West, I hate to inform you of this, but you're slaughtering these wee packages. Just what have you done here?"

"It's the corners that get me," I said with a sigh. "I think I have it neatly lined up, but then it all falls apart."

"I suppose that's the nature of life, isn't it. Well, let me get on with it," Maisie said, a note of determination in her voice, and I stepped back to let her do her work. Taking the books that were wrapped, I placed them strategically around the wide table, making sure there would be enough room for the rings to land on small pillars we placed on top. Still, I needed to test the throwing distance.

"Fancy a go?" I asked, tilting my head at Maisie, and she turned to see me holding the rings. Her eyes lit. Well, that was one way to get her to do something, I realized, and filed that note away for another time.

"What are we playing for?"

"Dinner."

"As in who is paying or if I'll go with you?" Maisie asked and my heart did a little dance. This meant she'd already decided to have dinner with me but hadn't told me yet. I wasn't sure she knew what she'd revealed to me, so I tucked my smile away.

"Who pays," I said, just because I knew it would heighten the stakes and she was unintentionally already agreeing to a date with me.

"Bring it on," Maisie said, stepping behind the line that I'd taped on the floor. I'd looked up the suggested distance for ring toss on my phone and then adjusted it slightly so it wasn't too difficult for people to win. This was a Christmas festival after all. There should be some good spirit involved.

"Toss for toss?" I asked, holding up my rings.

"Sure." Maisie pursed her lips, judging the distance from the tape to the table, while I made my first throw. The ring landed, but bounced off the table and didn't land on the pillar.

"Damn."

Maisie stepped up. Her face was set in fierce lines, all determination and focus. I *wanted to be on the receiving end of that look.* What would she look like after I made love to her? *Slowly and with great attention to detail.* Would her skin flush that pretty pink I'd seen last night when I'd caught her staring at me?

"Yes!" Maisie crowed, wiggling her butt in a little victory dance, and I turned to see her ring around one of the pillars.

"Nice shot. I guess I'll have to up my game." I tossed my next ring while looking at her and not the table and was rewarded when her face flashed with annoyance.

"Unbelievable. Were you just holding out on me? Have you been practicing?" I'd shaken Maisie enough that she'd missed her next toss and we were tied.

"Lucky throw," I assured her, hefting the last ring in my hand.

"I'm very tempted to distract you right now," Maisie grumbled.

"You're too competitive to cheat." But she'd already distracted me, just by being there, and my last ring caught the edge of a book, teetered, and fell to the floor.

"Yes! Okay, okay, okay. Focus, Maisie." Maisie closed her eyes and took a deep breath before tossing her ring. We both watched it soar through the air and land neatly around one of the pillars. "Yes!"

Maisie jumped up and down and I caught her in a hug, laughing as she danced in my arms. I wanted so badly to kiss her in that moment but wasn't sure if she'd be happy with me doing so in front of all of Loren Brae. To be respectful, I let her go.

"It's a date, then," I said, bowing and acknowledging my defeat.

"A date." Maisie shook her head. "It's been a bit since I've gone on an actual date. When was your last date?"

"Ah, well ..." I trailed off. I hadn't dated anyone since my ex-girlfriend, instead having taken time off to just make sure I had my head on straight before I gave it a go with another woman. It had been at least about a year and a half, if my calculations were correct.

"That long, huh? I'm surprised. Dr. Sexy Storybooks and all that," Maisie said. "Bad breakup?"

"Something like that."

When Maisie just looked at me, waiting for more, I sighed and rubbed a hand across my face. While I dearly didn't want to discuss my ex, it was only fair that the woman that I hoped to have a future with would know my past. Even if she didn't yet know there was a future for us.

"My ex-girlfriend and I dated for four years, and well ..."

"She cheated?" Maisie asked, returning to wrapping the books while I cut off pieces of tape for her.

"Nope. Well, not that I know of."

"You cheated?" This was said with a note of disbelief, so at least that pleased me.

"Never." I laughed. "Not my style."

"Thought so. You seem like a play by the rules type of guy."

"I've been known to break them when the time is right," I said as I tucked a wayward curl behind her ear and let my finger trace lightly down her neck. She shivered under my touch, and I grinned when I saw the telltale flush at her cheeks.

"So no cheating. What happened then?"

"She loved her career more than she loved me." It still

hurt to say it. I'd wanted so badly for her to choose me, not *instead* of her career, but I also didn't want to be an afterthought in her life. I'd spent enough of my life hidden behind books, I didn't want to disappear to my partner as well. "I guess she just fell out of love with me. Or we fell out of love with each other, I suppose. We grew apart. Her life was just so …" I tilted my head as I thought about my wild child of an ex-girlfriend. "She was—*is*—I guess, quite famous, and it just didn't align with my life. Or I didn't fit with hers."

At that, Maisie stopped wrapping and turned to me, her mouth rounded in shock.

"You dated a famous person? Who?" Maisie demanded.

"I'm not sure you'd know her. She's quite popular in the States. She's a singer actually."

"And?" Maisie drew the word out and I stalled, not wanting to answer the inevitable barrage of questions I often got once people learned that I'd dated a famous singer.

"Her name is CeeCee Rhodes. She's—"

"You dated CeeCee freaking Rhodes?" Maisie cried, and I motioned to her to keep her voice down. "Sorry, sorry. But. Oh my God, West. She's, like, *huge*. And beautiful. And her voice …"

"Yes, yes, she's all of those things," I agreed, keeping my voice low as a few people glanced our way.

"And you broke up with her?" Maisie whispered in surprise.

"Well, she broke up with me. But it was for the best. She's touring constantly and we never saw each other. Her career mattered more than I did. I can't say I blame her, either. Her star was rising, and she couldn't balance a relationship along with it. There's no bad blood or anything. But I just needed some time to get my head on straight after, I guess."

"And how long ago was this?" Maisie's voice held a tone I couldn't quite pin down.

"About a year and a half ago," I said. "Perhaps just a bit longer? Around that."

"And you've dated nobody since?"

"No, I've been really busy with work, and I just was focusing on myself."

"No one-night stand to scratch an itch? To shake it off?"

"I can scratch my own itch if needed." I smiled at that. "I wasn't in the headspace for dating. Now I am."

"So I'd be the first since—"

At that Maisie clamped her lips shut and understanding dawned. She was jealous of my ex-girlfriend. Which meant she was already thinking past our date to what would happen next. Delighted at this turn of events, I sought to soothe her worries.

"First what, love?"

"Oh wheesht," Maisie said, gathering a stack of books in her arms. "Don't make me say it."

"Oh, but I'd dearly love to know what you were thinking." Amusement danced through me. As if on cue, the Christmas music playing in the background turned to a song covered by CeeCee and Maisie glared at the ceiling of the tent.

"Seriously?" Maisie griped.

"Listen, Maisie." I pulled the books from her hands and

gripped her shoulders, forcing her to look at me. I didn't care who was watching because this was more important. "I'm not going to say bad things about my ex-girlfriend. She's a lovely person. But we wanted different things in life. While I hold fondness and respect for her, I'm no longer in love with CeeCee. I don't think about her, I don't crave her lifestyle, and I don't miss being with her. Yes, the breakup hurt my feelings. Which it should. I wouldn't have been with her for four years if I hadn't cared about her. But I've moved through those feelings. She was a part of my life, and now no longer is."

Maisie looked somewhat mollified.

"I don't suppose you could get me tickets to a concert?"

At that, I laughed and slung my arm around her shoulder.

"Absolutely not. Now, it's time to open. Look at that line. We're going to have a busy day ahead of us."

The hours passed in a blur, and I couldn't believe how many people had come out to visit the festival. Our booth was a crowd favorite, and between wrapping more books, selling tickets, and collecting rings, I barely had a chance to look up. Toward mid-afternoon though, I noticed a perceptible shift in the crowd, as laughter and conversation turned to concerned voices.

When the Christmas music cut out, I stopped and looked at Maisie.

"Is something going on?"

"I'm not sure." Maisie shrugged and we turned at a shout. In the front of the hall, we saw Agnes standing on a picnic table, waving her hands.

"Everyone! Hello! Yes, yes, please listen up. Unfortunately, we're going to have to cut the festival short. It appears that a serious blizzard is on the way, and the authorities have issued an emergency order. Everyone must return to their homes or accommodations as quickly as possible. For those who have traveled far and don't want to risk driving, please head to MacAlpine Castle."

The crowd reacted with astonishment, and I turned to Maisie with surprise.

"I didn't know that Loren Brae got this much snow."

"We typically don't." Maisie had a dumbstruck look on her face.

"Well, let's get things packed up before we head out. I don't want to leave them dealing with this."

For the next half hour, we worked at a rapid pace, following shouted orders, as the wind picked up and snow began to fall.

"West, we can't wait any longer."

I turned at Esther's voice, noting the worried looks on the Book Bitches' faces, and realized they were waiting to give me a ride back to my cottage.

"Oh, I can walk—"

"No, mate. Go with them. We can't stress the authorities with anyone getting stuck in this. It's coming in fast and furious. Let us know when you get in." Lachlan appeared at my side, his face set in worried lines, and I realized he had a lot on his shoulders as he was the castle caretaker and would be dealing with any stranded guests.

"Have you seen Maisie?" I asked, looking around.

"She's gone back to Bonnie Books with a load of boxes. Agnes is with her."

"So long as she is safe. Tell her I left then?"

"Will do."

As much as I knew the Book Bitches would want me to say goodbye to Maisie, their safety was more important. Following them to the car, we all clambered in, and Shannon took off at a careful pace. At the moment, the snow was falling in that picturesque way that made it look like you were inside a snow globe. Chunky snowflakes fell from the sky, the wind picking them up and twirling them across the serene waters of the loch. The roads were still clear enough, and we followed a long line of cars that departed Loren Brae.

"Such a shame," Esther said, clucking her tongue. "It was a cracking festival, wasn't it?"

"Where are you ladies staying? You won't try to go home, will you?"

"No, that's too far. We'll tuck in at our lovely wee inn and read some of our new books, won't we, ladies?" Cherise asked.

"It's just another ten minutes up the road from you," Shannon reassured me, seeing my look of worry even though the weather wasn't terrible quite yet. "This isn't our first weather event in Scotland, you ken?"

"A blizzard is not usual for this area though," Esther said.

"No, not particularly, but we'll weather it just fine, won't we, ladies? It's you we're worried about. You know how to stock your fireplace? We put food in your fridge, so you'll be fine there. Look for candles and flashlights in case the power goes out," Cherise said, lecturing me, and I nodded.

"Thanks, ladies. I'll be sure to take the proper precautions."

They pulled to a stop at my cottage, and I got out, waving goodbye as they left quickly. Standing for a moment, I faced the loch, and the wind blasted me, a warning of what was to come.

The ladies were right. I'd better get things in place and bring in wood from the woodpile. It was smart to be prepared. Granted, I'd never dealt with something like this in California, but I wasn't stupid, and I had Google as my friend. Surely I'd figure it out.

CHAPTER TEN

Maisie

The snow falling in the soft glow of the streetlight looked like someone had ripped up a box of printer paper and tossed it in front of a high-powered fan. It whipped around in circles before dropping to the ground and I bit my lip as I watched from the window at Agnes's flat.

I should have gotten West's number.

I was bummed that I'd missed him leave, but I understood that in the flurry of breaking down the festival he needed to take a ride back to his cottage. But now, I couldn't help but worry about him, out there in the cold and not used to these conditions.

The snow clung to the streets, a soft blanket of white, with no tire tracks to mar the pristine landscape.

"You should go to him."

"What? I wasn't—" I whirled, looking to where Agnes

stood in my bedroom doorway with her cozy house slippers on, holding a cup of tea.

"You were. You should go. You've got a truck."

I did have a truck. With four-wheel drive. It was a country girl's truck and had come in useful on more than one occasion.

"I don't know, Agnes. It's really coming down out there. What if I get stuck?" I turned back to study the roads. The snow wasn't horribly high, yet. But driving in these conditions would be like driving blind. Surely it wasn't safe.

"You won't and if you do, Graham and I will come get you."

"I don't want to leave you alone."

"I'm not alone." Agnes gestured with her cup to The Tipsy Thistle across the street. "Graham's right there. And a few stragglers have already gone to the pub. If I need help, I can certainly cross the street and get it. Weston, on the other hand, is all alone in the middle of nowhere in the biggest weather event this town may likely ever see."

The forecast was calling for almost two feet of snow, which was beyond anything we'd ever experienced before, and forecasters warned of drifts that could get higher than our heads. I nibbled my bottom lip, torn. It would be stupid to go out there, wouldn't it?

"I wouldn't delay much longer, or you will be well and truly out of choices."

Thinking of West all alone in the cottage, maybe not knowing how to use his fireplace, spurred me into action. Grabbing an extra jumper, I pulled it over my head, along with my heavy coat, gloves, hat, and waterproof hiking boots. Spying my phone and charger, I grabbed both and put them in a bag, as well as my laptop.

"Here, take these just in case." Agnes handed me a box of candles, matches, and a flashlight. In her other hand, she offered a market bag. "Rations, if needed. Oh, and I added a power bank to charge phones too."

"You won't need it?" I stopped and Agnes shook her head.

"I sell them at the store. I have a few charging now, so even if the power goes out, I'll be able to fully charge anything I need for days."

"Okay, be safe." I gave her a hug and she held on to me for an extra few seconds.

"Drive very slowly. Try to look down at the road and not at the oncoming snow. Look for other headlights coming your way. Don't slam on your brakes."

"Will do."

I'd driven in the snow plenty of times, but this would be the most intense. Even as I stepped outside, my stomach dropped. There was a silence to the town, like someone had muffled Loren Brae, and I stared in awe at the snow that swirled around me. Agnes was right, I'd better get moving if I had any chance of reaching West. Hoping I wasn't making a huge mistake, I hopped into my truck parked at the curb and turned on the windshield wipers to scrape off the snow that had already accumulated. Once I'd let the truck warm up a bit, I put it into four-wheel drive, shifted into gear, and slowly drove down the main street.

It was somewhat incredible, seeing the village like this, lights shining softly beneath heavy sheets of snow. My truck, to my relief, handled the snow fairly easily, though I did have a few moments where it slid as I got used to being gentle with the brakes. Turning left from the quiet town, I held my breath as I drove onto the road that hugged Loch Mirren. At least there was an easy demarcation point between where the water was and the road, and with no other oncoming cars that I could see, I inched slowly along, praying that nothing would cause me to slam on my brakes and slide into the freezing water.

"Go slow, go slow, go slow," I ordered myself. It was almost hypnotizing, the way the snow came at the headlights, reminding me of the beginning of Star Wars when they went into light speed. The minutes crept by as I made progress, my hands clenching the wheel tightly.

"I swear to God, Clyde, if you jump out in front of me right now I will never, *ever*, laugh at one of your stupid coo jokes again," I warned. Thankfully the road remained clear. By the time I neared West's cottage, a light sweat had broken out on my brow as the snow had intensified, and my truck was starting to struggle. When I saw the light at his front door, I let out a sigh of relief. Even if I had to stop now, I'd be able to walk to his cottage. Luckily, my truck made it just far enough to pull into the driveway next to his cottage before promptly sliding into a snowbank with a cheerful crunch.

"Oh, shit. Please be home." I suddenly realized that there was a possibility that Matthew had come to collect West and he might be at the castle with everyone else who had gotten stranded. If so, then I may have just made a dangerous situation even worse. My heart hammered in my chest as I grabbed the bags and stumbled through the snow, gasping for breath by the time I reached the cottage door. I was just raising my hand to knock when the door opened, and I fell through it into a startled West's arms. "Oh thank God, you're here."

"Maisie? What are you doing here?" West asked, pulling me inside and slamming the door against the wind that screamed at my back. Even in just the walk from the truck to the cottage, I was fully coated in a layer of chunky snowflakes. "You look like the abominable snowman."

"I …" I gasped and held up my hand, needing a moment to calm myself as adrenaline shook my body. Now that the drive was over, I realized just how intense it had been.

"Here, let me get this off you." West pulled the bags from my hands and unzipped my coat. In a matter of moments, he had me stripped down to my long underwear and jumper, hanging my dripping garments over the backs of the kitchen chairs. As I caught my breath, I saw a fire crackling merrily in the fireplace and was grateful to see that no smoke came back into the cottage. At least he knew enough to open the flue.

Then he stepped back and gave me such a smug grin that I lifted my chin.

"What is *that* look for?" I demanded.

"You came for me."

I'd like to …

Pushing that thought away, I glared at him.

"Yeah, because I was certain you'd probably die up here all by yourself not used to snowstorms."

"You like me." West said it in a sing-songy voice, and I rolled my eyes.

"Don't be so full of yourself." I huffed. "We can't have needless deaths at the Book Festival. It's bad for tourism."

"You were worried about me."

"If you'd just given me your phone number, then I could have texted you to make sure you were safe."

"Ah, now she wants my phone number."

"I can leave, you know." I pointed back at the door. Now probably wasn't the time to tell him that my truck was stuck in a large snowbank in his driveway.

"After all that hard work? We can't let a knight in shining armor not have the spoils of her win now, can we? Come in, come in. As you can see, I was just settling by the fire."

"Let me just put this food in the fridge and text Agnes that I'm here."

"You brought rations? See, you are sweet on me." West grinned when I snarled at him and stomped to the fridge, only to open it and see it fully stocked.

"Well, it looks like this wasn't needed."

"The Book Bitches hooked me up this morning. While they are the scariest group of women I've ever met, apparently they also will mother the hell out of you with brute force. They attacked me at seven this morning, cooked me breakfast, and stocked my fridge with food. It was a dizzying experience."

"I can imagine." Despite myself I smiled, though nerves still skittered low in my stomach. Now that I was here, I was beginning to understand the predicament that I'd put myself in. It wasn't likely that I was going anywhere tonight. So here we were. In a cottage. Snowed in together.

"Can I pour you a glass of wine? I've just opened a lovely red."

"Please," I said. Perhaps it would calm my nerves.

West poured a glass, and I followed him to the couch by the fire, scanning the cottage. West had turned the other lights low, and the light from the flames flickered over the wooden beams in the ceiling and the pretty stone walls. A rug with intricate woven patterns in reds and soft greys was tossed across the worn wood floor in front of the fire. On one of the side tables were a stack of artsy books and a deck of cards.

"This place is really nice."

"It's cozy, isn't it? It even has a wood-burning hot tub, though I've been reluctant to give it a go."

"Is that right? You do need to get the wood burning well before you want to go in to give it some time to heat up."

"Do you have one?"

"A hot tub?" I laughed and settled onto one side of the couch and West took the other. "I wish. But I secretly love them. Whenever I get a chance to go on a mini holiday, I always try to book a place with a hot tub. It's always so cold here that it just adds an extra layer of coziness to a stay."

"What's your place like?"

"Where I live you mean?"

West nodded, and I tilted my head at him, wondering how to explain to this man who dated famous people that I lived in a studio flat and walked most days to work to save on petrol.

"It's a very small, serviceable studio flat. It's tiny, but charming, and I make do. The rent is affordable and it's close to work."

"And are you thinking about transitioning to being a full-time author?"

"No." I rolled my eyes. "You know that I haven't sold anything yet."

"That doesn't mean you can't think about what that life might look like someday."

"True, I suppose. No, I mostly enjoy my work at the post office. I'm the manager and it's the main hub for our wee town. It's almost more of a general store really."

"That sounds fun, if you enjoy it. Then maybe there's a way to continue to do both if you wanted to?"

I blinked at him, studying his face for any hint of sarcasm, but found none. I thought about his question. Did I enjoy my work? I'd always just worked there because it was a steady job.

"I don't *not* enjoy it. Some days are better than others. It's not what I saw for myself, I guess."

"But writing is. Tell me more about your novel."

"I …" I glanced down at the deck of cards sitting on top of a small cribbage board, feeling anxious as he so casually brought up one of my most long-held dreams. "Do you want to play cards?"

"Sure." West reached for the cards and the cribbage board tucked beneath them and handed them to me. "Dealer's choice."

"Do you know cribbage?"

"Of course."

"Great." I shuffled the cards while West stayed silent. I knew there wasn't any escaping his question. "It's about a girl who discovers if she picks up objects, she can see the last person who held them."

"Psychometry." West nodded.

"Aye, and so when her boyfriend goes missing, the

police look to her. But she knows, by holding his car keys, that he was actually trying to frame her to cover up illegal weapons trafficking that she had no knowledge of. But it's a small town with kind of an old boys' club, and the men are partial to believing the other men. She's out on bail but time is ticking to prove her innocence while also not getting killed by her boyfriend in the meantime. For added spice, the detective falls for her."

"Intense." West's grin was so wide that I stopped shuffling and stared at him.

"What?"

"I love it. I think it's got an interesting hook, and the potential for a lot of twists and turns. Will you let me read it?"

Would I let a professor of literature read my amateur mystery novel? *Hell-to-the-no*.

"No."

"Why not?" West tilted his head at me. When I didn't answer, he reached out and nudged me with his foot. "Why, Maisie?"

"You're a professor. I'm not … this is just … it's not there yet."

"Writing a book is a huge accomplishment, Maisie. You should be proud of yourself. And I read my students' work every day. It's literally part of my job. I'm well aware of being sensitive to feelings and also offering constructive feedback. Trust me, I'd be a lot nicer with my insights than a lot of agents will be."

The man had a point.

"Maybe. I'll think about it."

"I bet it's better than you think."

The idea of other eyes on my work made me squeamish, and at the same time, wasn't that what I was trying to achieve with submitting my manuscript to countless agents? I squirmed under West's assessing gaze, certain he saw too much of my soul, his nearness both arousing and unsettling me. I was used to people looking past me, just another thread in the fabric of the town, and to have someone see *me*, the real me, was disconcerting. *Maybe that was a good thing.*

"What are we playing for?" I asked, pointing to the cards.

"Winner's choice?"

"No way, you have to declare it first," I argued. Leaning back, I took a sip of my wine.

"Fine, you go."

"Okay. If I win, you have to go out and start the hot tub."

"You'd send me to my death in a blizzard?" West held a hand to his heart, and I giggled.

"It can't be that far away."

"I'm just a poor California boy with thin blood." West mocked shivering, and I kicked him lightly.

"Then don't lose."

"Fine. It's on."

I grinned to myself. The man had no way of knowing that I played a killer game of cribbage, and when the game ended with me as the winner, his face fell in defeat.

"I can't believe I lost. I'm not typically horrible at this game."

"Good to know. Better suit up." I laughed as West grumbled, but in solidarity, I pulled my damp jeans on, put my jacket over my jumper, and slid my feet into the boots. Flipping on the outdoor light, we both peered into the blizzard.

"Oh, perfect," I sighed in happiness, imagining slipping into the hot water later in the evening. "Look at how well it's sheltered under the alcove there. The snow's all piling up on the other side."

"Yes, just a lovely quiet evening," West grumbled, and I laughed.

"You won't need a ton of wood to get it going. Just a few logs and some tinder. Then you'll keep checking it every half hour or so."

"Every half hour ..." West glared at me.

"Don't be a sore loser," I lectured.

By the time he'd made it through the snow, started the fire in the attached enclosed wood burner, and returned to the cottage, West was positively coated in snow. I couldn't help myself and snorted as his glasses fogged the moment he stepped inside the cottage.

"Here, let me get those for you." I slid them off his face, caught once more on his gorgeous eyes, and held them while he rid himself of his snowy clothes.

"I think you've lost your mind if you believe going in that tub is going to be fun tonight."

"It might be. It's nice to have options, isn't it?" I handed him his glasses once he was down to his jeans and sweater, and he pulled a handkerchief from his pocket to carefully dry them off. My heart melted. The man carried a hanky, loved books, and played a serviceable game of cribbage. *And* was drop-dead gorgeous. How any woman could fall out of love with him was a mystery to me. I was still feeling stupefied over knowing that this man had dated CeeCee Rhodes. She was not only stunning, but so, so successful. *Why would West want to be with someone like me? After her?*

"Another round?" West asked.

I would never say no to another game and happily snuggled back on the couch after he'd topped off my glass of wine.

"You get to choose what we are playing for this time," I said, magnanimous in my victory.

"Perfect. If I win, you'll email me your manuscript. Tonight."

My mouth dropped open. That wee sneak. No way was he winning my book.

"Fine. But based on how you just played, I think that's a bold ask, isn't it?"

"We gotta take risks, don't we, Maisie?" West looked at me, and I shivered under the double meaning of his words.

"Fine. Shuffle." I bent to the deck, so determined to win that we didn't even talk this round like we had on the last game. By the time we neared the last turn and headed toward the final points, panic gripped me. West was ahead by five points, and he counted his hand first. I just needed him to have *less* than five points. I'd been too tense to count the points in his hand as we'd played the last hand and my stomach sunk as his grin widened.

"Good game, Maisie." West picked up his peg and put it in the winning hole and I gaped down at the board.

"I can't believe I lost." Seriously, I wasn't enjoying this new trend of losing games. Maybe it was West's sexiness that was distracting me?

A KILT FOR CHRISTMAS

"Pay up." West pointed at my phone.

"It's on my laptop." I stalled.

"Good thing you brought it with you then."

Damn it. I'd forgotten I'd unpacked my bags and put the computer on the counter. Sighing, I stood and went to my computer, and turned it on.

"Sorry, no Wi-Fi," I said.

"Here's the code," West said over my shoulder, and I jumped at his nearness. Annoyed, I entered the code, surprised the Internet still worked in this blizzard, and entered his email address. When it was done, I whirled and crossed my arms over my chest.

"You'd better be nice about it."

"I'm always nice." West grinned, caging me in at the bar, his hands on either side of me. Heat licked up my body. "Thank you for sharing it with me. I promise to treat it with the utmost care."

"You'd better," I muttered.

"I will. Promise." West leaned down and brushed his lips over mine, sealing his promise with a gentle kiss before stepping back. His eyes softened at the dazed look on my face. Capturing my chin with his hand, West bent and took my lips once more, desire blooming inside of me as he masterfully commanded the kiss until all I could think about was having him use that single-minded focus on my body in the bedroom. There was something to be said for a man who could focus so intently on the task at hand that all thoughts fled my brain except the deep need for *more*. When he finally broke the kiss and stepped back, a chill brushed my skin, and I immediately missed his nearness.

"It's time for me to put wood in."

I blinked at him, taking a moment to realize he meant the fire, and my cheeks flamed. *Yes, please.* Would it be crass to beg? Guessing correctly at my thoughts, West threw his head back and laughed. Flicking a finger down my cheek, he nodded at the door.

"The hot tub."

"Yes, yes, I got it. Can I use your bathroom?"

"Sure thing, through the bedroom." West turned to suit up, and I beelined for his bathroom and confirmed in the mirror above the sink that my face, indeed, was on fire. What was I doing here, with him? I felt like I was a snowball rolling downhill, caught under a force I didn't quite understand. It was heady, and unsettling, and exciting all the same. But ... what could he possibly see in me after dating CeeCee of all people? Making a stern face in the mirror, I held a finger up to lecture myself.

"You don't need to be famous to be a great catch, Maisie. You're a damn good person, reasonably good-looking, and you're smart. Anybody would consider you a catch." It wasn't the first time I'd given myself wee pep talks in the mirror, typically after another rejection email came back on my manuscript, and it had become like a wee ceremony of mine to splash water on my face and crack on with life. Sometimes, I'd make myself laugh, feeling like a teenage boy flexing his muscles in the mirror, but there was something to be said for a few positive words to shore up waning confidence.

Once my confidence-boost was done, I splashed some water on my face to cool my heated cheeks and came back in time to see West shaking off the snow at the door.

"It's really coming down out there, I've never seen anything like it."

His words shook something loose in my brain and my eyes widened.

My phone pinged before I could speak, and I checked a message from Agnes.

Whatever you do, stay where you are. This is the worst blizzard to ever hit the area. We're about to have the snowiest Christmas ever.

Guilt flashed through me, and West came to my side, wiping his glasses.

"What's up?"

"I ... I think this is my fault."

"Please be more specific."

"The blizzard."

West laughed and slid his glasses back on. "While I do think you are a goddess, even you can't control the weather."

Wait ... he thinks I'm a goddess?

"No ..." I shook my head, focusing. "You don't understand. At the stones. That was my wish. I'd wished for the snowiest Christmas ever."

CHAPTER ELEVEN

Maisie

West pulled me to the couch and settled me next to him.

"I thought you didn't believe in the Christmas Wish."

I looked at him helplessly. Standing up, he added more wood to the dwindling fire, and the crackling of fresh logs filled the silence in the room. Once he returned to the couch, he took my hand and began to massage my palm.

"I don't. I didn't. But ..." I gestured to the windows.

"Yes, this does seem to indicate there's truth in the power of the stones," West agreed, pressing his lips together as he continued to massage. "Which, given the historical nature of the mystical elements surrounding most standing stones, it would track with previous accounts."

"You're saying that this is all my fault?"

"*I'm* just agreeing with the conclusion that you yourself have reached," West amended.

"Oh God, I hope nobody gets hurt."

"Hopefully they got the warning out soon enough. Don't worry. It will be okay. It's not like this area doesn't get snow, so most people will be prepared, right?"

"True. But still. I feel horrible. I had no idea that a simple wish could turn into—"

"The blizzard of the century?" West teased.

"Wheesht." I smacked his arm lightly.

"Come on, let's play another game. Take your mind off things until you go in the hot tub."

"Until *we* go in the hot tub," I amended, reaching for the cards.

"Woman. It is freezing out there. If you think I'm going in the hot tub, you've lost your mind."

"Wanna bet?" I brandished the cards.

"What are we playing?" West asked.

"Poker."

"Strip poker," West suggested, and I laughed.

"I suspect California boy's gonna get real cold, real quick."

West pursed his lips as he thought about it.

"You're not wrong. As much as I'd deeply love to see that luscious body of yours in just your skivvies, I can't imagine it will be all that fun to sit here half-naked. Even with the fire, it's still chilly in here."

"What makes you think I'd be the one stripping down?" I gave West a challenging look and he flashed me a feral grin that had my insides going liquid.

"I'm reward motivated. I'd have you out of your clothes in a matter of rounds."

He could have me out of my clothes right now if he

wanted to. But I just managed to restrain myself from saying *that* particular thought.

"As much as I hate to wipe that confident smirk off your face, it's really in your best interest not to play me. I'd hate for you to catch a cold."

"Another time then," West acquiesced, and the casual way he spoke of a future date together made my heart sing.

"Smart man." I sighed happily as West switched hands. "Tell me about California. Your place. Your job. What's your life like there? It feels so magical and far away. Everyone always talks about California here like it's all sunshine and having dinner with movie stars every night. Well, I guess I suppose that was what it was for you, wasn't it? With your ex?"

"I did meet some famous people through her, yes, but largely speaking, there's only the occasional celebrity sighting when you're at the supermarket."

"Get out. When you're at the market? How exciting! I feel like I'd be stalking the markets just to see someone famous. Who was your most interesting famous person?" Aside from your ex-girlfriend, I silently added.

"I saw Harry Styles buying a green juice at Whole Foods."

"Stop it," I breathed.

"Seriously. The poor guy was surrounded as soon as people recognized him. Luckily, I was near an exit and whistled for him to use the door. He even thanked me as he breezed by."

"What did he smell like?" I asked dreamily and West raised an eyebrow.

"You think that I leaned in to ... *smell* him?"

"I mean, if he walked past you through a door, maybe you—" I giggled at West's stormy expression.

"Do you have a crush on Harry Styles?"

"Gosh, who doesn't? The man has charisma."

"He does, in spades. Unfortunately, or fortunately, depending how you look at it, I am unable to report on the signature scent of one said Harry Styles, but I'm sure you could look online if needed and spritz your pillow with it each night while falling asleep to his smooth vocal stylings."

"Good call. I should go look it up now." I pretended to reach for my phone and gasped in laughter when West pounced, pulling me on top of him.

"You will not," West said, dropping a kiss casually on my lips. He was so easy with me, cuddling me like I was his girlfriend or something, and I wanted to snuggle into him and never let go. "Now, to answer your question, I have a love/hate relationship with California. I love living near the water, I'm pretty stoked about the sunshine, but the people are a mixed bag. Some are super chill, easygoing surfer types, and others are really involved in all things Hollywood, which at times can come across quite fake. It's a tricky landscape to navigate because everyone always seems to have a hidden agenda. Luckily, at the university, I'm largely away from most of that."

"And you like teaching?" I asked, turning so my head rested on his chest and he wrapped his arms more tightly around me.

"I do. Mostly. It wasn't what I'd thought I'd get into. I'd always thought I'd write sweeping novels that would bring the nation to tears."

"You want to be a writer as well?" I tilted my head to look up at him. His lips creased in a wry smile.

"I do. But you have more courage than I do, Maisie. You've gone and done what I haven't been able to bring myself to do yet. You've written your novel, which is why I'm so very proud of you."

"You'll get there. If you want it bad enough," I said, surprised that I was the one offering him support. He seemed so accomplished to me.

"I think I just might." West's laugh rumbled in his chest. "Otherwise, I've been living with two roommates from hell and am overly delighted that when I go home, I'll be getting the keys to a new place for just myself. It's a dream come true."

"You have roommates?" For some reason, this really surprised me. I was picturing him in some palatial house overlooking the ocean with bikini-clad women strolling by in front of his house.

"Real estate in California is horribly expensive. As is the cost of living. It just made economical sense."

The idea that he was frugal with his money charmed me, as I had always had to be as well. It was a small thing, maybe, but finding this commonality, along with his love of writing, made me feel so much more connected to this man.

I jolted as an alarm went off.

"Time to check the hot tub."

I almost stopped him, wanting to just snuggle into his chest a moment longer, but it wouldn't be fair of me to force him out into the blizzard and not actually use the hot tub. For better or worse, it looked like we were going in the tub.

Yes, *we*.

West didn't know it yet, but he would absolutely be joining me in the tub.

"It should be warm enough now," I said, checking the clock. "Are you ready to go in?"

"Go in, she says. Like there isn't a monstrous storm the likes of which Loren Brae has never seen before going on outside."

"It may be awful. It may be awesome. We gotta take risks, don't we, West?" I mimicked his earlier words and he glared at me.

We both went to the door and peered out. The storm had somewhat abated, the snowflakes coming down in lazy swirls in the light from the porch, and West turned to look down at me.

"You're really going to make me do this, aren't you?"

"I'm not going to make you do anything. But I'm going in." Grabbing a blanket from a basket of throw blankets by the couch, I held it up.

"And just what do you plan on wearing to go in? I can't imagine you've packed your bathing suit this fine winter's evening."

"Well, West, you see, we humans come with a built-in bathing costume called our skin." I peeled off my jumper to stand in just my underpants and T-shirt before him. He gaped at me and I made a motion with my finger. "Turn around."

Dutifully West turned and I stripped, giggling as he swallowed audibly, and then wrapped the blanket around me like a towel. Tugging my boots on, I walked over to the door.

"Care to get the cover off for me?"

"I think you know exactly what you're doing," West said, pulling on his coat and trudging out into the snow. Dusting the snow off the top of the cover, he tugged it off and leaned on the side of the alcove that was collecting the least amount of snow, and then turned to glare at me. "Well, then, come on, princess."

Giggling, I ran out into the snow, the shock of the cold on my bare skin making my breath catch, and I took his hand at the side of the tub. He turned away, and I took the blanket off, putting it on the edge of the tub, and climbed quickly inside, the steam from the heated water hitting the cold air concealing my nakedness. The shock of the hot water had my skin burning for a moment before I adjusted to the temperature, and I was immensely pleased with just how well the tub had heated.

"Well, then. You enjoy yourself. Call me when you need help getting out," West said primly, trudging back toward the door, and I laughed even harder.

"It's nice and hot in here, West. Are you sure you can't handle a wee bit of cold?"

"I'm trying to be polite here, Maisie, but you're making it very hard for me to maintain being a gentleman."

"Who said I wanted you to be a gentleman?" Far from it, if anything. I wanted to ruffle his feathers, see him unsettled, because thus far he'd been so perfectly even keeled that I still didn't know what would make him come undone.

Silence met my words, and I just shrugged, leaning my shoulders back and luxuriating in the hot water that soothed my muscles. The night sky was covered in murky clouds, and snow drifted down, wee droplets of icy cold on my cheeks, which were instantly melted by the steam from the water. These were all of my favorite things coming together at once. The snow falling mixed with the pleasure of soaking in a decadent hot tub, a glass of wine at my side. The one thing that would make this better? I wanted, desperately, for West to join me. Just the thought of his all-consuming kisses, his body brushing against mine in the water, the sharp contrast of icy snow on heated skin—

"I thought you'd learned to be careful what you wished for."

West's voice at my ear made me jump. He'd moved so quietly through the snow that I hadn't even heard his approach and now I gaped as he climbed into the hot tub and reached for me, pulling me with my back to his chest and holding me tightly against him.

"West," I gasped, as he scraped his teeth along my shoulder, nibbling at the delicate skin there as his hands stroked lazily down my sides and over the tops of my thighs. Unbidden, my legs dropped open at his touch, and I squirmed against him, heat flaring inside of me.

"Yes, Maisie? Is there something you're needing on this insanely cold evening?" West grumbled at my neck, and I found myself torn between laughter and a need so deep that my insides ached for his touch.

"Why yes, West, I'd very much like you to touch me all over until I can't think about anything else other than the pleasure you give me." I parroted back his precise tones.

"Your wish is my command."

I sighed as his hands cupped my breasts, massaging gently as they floated in the hot water, kneading them in his large palms. Moaning, I arched my back against his body, feeling how hard he was for me already, his hands methodically stroking me, as easily as he'd given me a hand massage earlier. Liquid heat pooled inside of me, and I rolled my body, rocking my hips against his hard length, needing, no, *aching* for more.

"Shhh, slow down, Maisie. We've got all night," West whispered at my neck, slowing his touch until he just caressed lazy circles on my stomach, and I wanted to scream. The pleasure had built so fast inside of me, from the sensation of his muscular body cocooning mine, the hot water surrounding us, and the icy wind at our faces, that I already thought I was going to explode. I tried to turn, deciding that I needed to take over, but he looped an arm around my waist, holding me in place. "Nope. I'm the one in control here."

His words sent a shiver through my whole body, and I couldn't quite connect this dominating side of West with the precise and polite professor I'd met so far. I suppose there had been hints. The way he'd caged me against the door and taken my mouth in the hottest kiss known to man. And now, when he danced his fingers up my inner thigh, tracing lazy figures of eight on the sensitive skin there while his other hand played lightly at my breast, I wanted to cry in frustration. Over and over, he stroked me everywhere except where I so desperately wanted to be touched, as though each part of my body was a new discovery to be explored. He paid careful attention to my ankles, the backs of my legs, the soft curve of my bottom. His hands danced a soft rhythm, soothing and stroking, toying lightly across my stomach, and tracing softly against where I wanted his touch most.

It was an aching, delightful, soul-searing kind of torture, as he relentlessly explored my body, all while whispering words of love in my ear.

"I've been wanting to touch you like this since the moment I met you."

I hissed in frustration.

"Before we even first kissed, at the stones, I already knew."

To my embarrassment, I mewled in distress.

"Sweet, Maisie, with the prettiest blue eyes I've ever seen, and a mouth made for kissing."

I was close to begging at this point.

"But do you know, darling Maisie, do you know what I ..." West trailed off and my brain short-circuited as he slid a finger below, finding my most sensitive spot, and sent a sharp wave of lust skyrocketing through my body. I arched against his hand, desperate for release, and he locked an arm around my waist again, holding me as I writhed with need. I shivered as his fingers played at my entrance, dipping in ever so slightly, his breath hot at my ear.

"West," I begged. He slid one finger inside me in one delicious stroke, all heat and wet and hard, and I shattered around his hand, waves of lust washing over me so that my body shook with my release. Crying out, I reared upward, needing the shock of the cold night air to soothe my body that blistered with need. In one swift movement, West turned me, so I straddled him, and teased me with his hard length.

I was beyond myself with need, riding the residual waves of lust that rocked my body, and I took his mouth in a searing kiss, needing that connection more than anything else I'd ever needed in my life. Snow drifted onto my back, icy drops cooling my flaming skin, and I moaned with need at his mouth. Pulling back, West gripped the back of my neck, forcing me to look at his eyes, as he positioned himself.

"Do you know what I wished for at the stones, Maisie?"

"What?" I gasped, my breath catching, my heart hammering in my chest.

"I wished for you to be mine."

My mouth dropped open in surprise as West entered me in one, long, delicious stroke, seating himself so thoroughly that I couldn't think of anything else but his hardness enveloped by all of my softness. It was like he'd been meant for me all along, filling me and fitting me, until there was nothing left to be hidden from him. Again that unsettling feeling of someone knowing all parts of me shook me, and when I went to pull back, he wrapped his arms around my shoulders and pulled my head down to his lips.

We stilled.

"Beautiful, stunning, prickly Maisie. Woman of my dreams. Goddess of my heart. When I first saw you in the pub, my entire world shifted, and then righted once more. You were like a hurricane, knocking my ship off course, only to discover that maybe you set me in the right direction all along."

"West," I breathed against his lips, my body pulsing gently around his, need building inside me along with something else so shimmering and beautiful that I feared it would shatter if I looked too deeply at what his words were doing to my heart, my soul, and my future. "I don't know what to say. Your words."

I clenched my hand at my chest, and West's hands followed suit, cupping my breasts, as I remained seated, the desire to move against his hard length almost killing me. There was something so erotic about being this close, but not moving, that was starting to drive me a little crazy. The tension inside me felt like a wire pulled too tight, ready to snap, and a soft cry of need escaped me as he devoted his attention to my sensitive breasts.

"Do you always need to have everything figured out ahead of time?" West asked, his tone conversational, as though he wasn't driving me crazy with his touch.

"I'm partial to it, yes." I gasped as I shifted my hips and he slid deeper, if that was even possible.

"Well then, just know that I'm not going anywhere, Maisie. I want to figure this out. With you. Whatever that takes."

His words split that shimmering inside of me open, and I reared back, no longer able to sit still. Clenching around him, baring myself to West's touch, I rode him into oblivion, with his chants of, "Mine, mine, mine," driving me over the edge into the sweetest abyss of pleasure that I'd ever known.

Collapsing against his chest, my head dipped under the hot water, and West pulled me up, turning me easily again so that he cradled me against his chest, and I took a moment to catch my breath. And to try and settle my emotions. Never before had I been with someone who had steadfastly and directly told me that they had wanted to be with me. It had always been a guessing game in the past, most ending in frustration and miscommunications, and now I wasn't sure what to do when a man like West told me he wanted me for his own. I ... well, I realized that I strangely liked it. Loved it, even. It was refreshing, this whole direct communication thing, and while I still didn't quite know what our future held, at the very least we had this moment.

West intertwined his fingers through mine, and we watched the snow swirl about in the light from the porch.

"Dream girl," West muttered at my ear, nipping lightly at the sensitive skin, and I giggled. Again, with the giggling.

"West ... I, well, we just live so far apart."

"We do. At the moment. But the beautiful thing about life is that we get to make our own choices."

I twisted in the water to look at him, my mouth hanging open at his cheeky grin. "What are you saying? You'd move to Scotland?"

"I don't know. I'm not saying that I wouldn't. But I'm not saying it's not a possibility. I'd need to gather more information. See if any universities are hiring, that kind of thing. Or you could come to California."

"Me? In Cali?" The idea wasn't entirely unwelcome, and I tried to imagine how quickly my pale Scottish skin would burn in the bright sunshine. "There's sunshine there."

"So I hear." West grinned and tugged me back so I was cradled against him once more and I let my eyes slide closed, enjoying this moment with him.

"Maisie."

"Mm-hmm?" I said, dreamily.

"Maisie." This time, West's tone of warning had me popping my eyes open. I gasped.

At the edge of the backyard, glowing of its own accord,

stood a luminous unicorn. Snow swirled around the majestic beast, shimmering, as though it had its own glitter halo. The unicorn dipped its head, pawing at the ground once, its horn shining a luminous pink, before it turned and trotted into the storm.

"Wait," I whispered, caught between tears and disbelief. I didn't want it to leave. What if it was cold? "Don't go. Are you safe?"

"I think, if it needed help, it would have let us know." West kissed the side of my neck, putting both arms around my waist as tears pricked my eyes.

"I can't believe ... that was the most beautiful thing I've ever seen in my life."

"That was the second most beautiful thing I've ever seen in my life. After you." At West's words my heart just melted into one big pile of puddly goo, and I sighed, leaning back into his arms as a million emotions raged inside of me.

"Told you that you'd like the hot tub," I said.

"Yes, you've enticed me over to the dark side. It's the getting out part I'm nervous about now."

"Oh yeah, that's the worst. You just have to scream the entire way and race for the shower."

"That's the preferred Scottish way?"

"Absolutely."

"Let's do it." West shrieked like a schoolgirl when his bare feet hit the snow, but he still turned to carry me so mine wouldn't. "This is not my favorite thing, Maisie."

"We'll toughen you up yet, West."

I laughed the whole way to the shower.

CHAPTER TWELVE

West

Time didn't seem to have any real meaning in a snowstorm, I realized, and we stayed up much of the night exploring each other's bodies before falling asleep in the early hours of the morning. I awoke, energized, long before Maisie and because I couldn't help myself, I curled up on the couch with my iPad, her manuscript, and a cup of coffee while the blizzard continued to rage outside. At this point, I was beginning to think that we weren't making it out of this cottage anytime soon and I, for one, didn't mind that.

Maisie slept through much of the morning, lightly snoring in bed, while I devoured her book. As a byproduct of my job, I was a fast reader, and by the time I'd finished it, it took everything in my power not to wake her up and tell her how absorbed I'd been. The character arcs were believable, it paced well, the tension was masterfully captured and maintained, the plot twist at eighty-five percent was ingenious, and I was captivated from the first to the last page. *This needs to be printed. She needs to be acknowledged.* And hopefully write more. Instead, I scrolled through my contacts to look for a literary agent friend of mine. For a moment, I hesitated, wondering if Maisie would be upset with me for sending her manuscript on. But she'd admitted she'd already sent it to over thirty agents, so I knew she was hoping to secure a contract. At the very least, it might be a connection that I could foster for her. Her book deserved a chance and if I could play a small part in making that happen, I was happy to do so. Without another thought, I dashed off an email to my friend and enclosed the manuscript. If he declined representation, I never had to say a word to Maisie about it.

"Good morning."

I glanced up to see a deliciously sleep-rumpled Maisie, wearing her long underwear and jumper, padding into the room. Immediately, I put my iPad aside and opened my arms and a look of relief briefly flashed across her face before she came to snuggle with me on the couch. I'd started the fire again this morning, and it crackled merrily, protecting us from the arctic cold outside.

"How'd you sleep?" I asked, holding her close, my heart rate increasing at her nearness. She fit with me, so perfectly, that I wanted to hold on and never let go. Already, my mind was considering what my future would look like, rearranging the picture that I'd had in my mind, and was rebuilding it with her by my side. I didn't care that we'd only just met. I knew, as sure as I knew that *Die Hard* was a Christmas movie, that we were meant for each other.

"Like a rock. What time is it anyway?" Maisie shifted

against me, and pulled back, standing to cross to the kitchen where her phone was plugged in at the wall. I immediately missed her presence. Following, I poured her a cup of coffee from the pot that I'd kept hot.

"I don't know how you take your coffee. But I do know how you take your men," I said, just to see that enticing pink flush flood her pretty face. When she glared at me, I laughed. Helpless not to, I tilted Maisie's face up to give her a lingering kiss.

"I like it sweet," Maisie admitted, when the kiss broke.

"Good to know."

Maisie's phone rang, and she answered immediately, nodding her thanks as I handed her the cup. Leaning back against the counter, I crossed my legs and watched as the snow continued to swirl outside. I could barely see the hot tub now, so it was a good thing we'd made use of it the night before. *And hell had it been a good use of our energy and time. Maisie, hot and wet, pressing against my body—*

"Oh no!" Maisie cried, and I shifted my attention to her panic-stricken face and crossed to her.

"What's wrong?" I asked, touching her shoulder lightly.

"The Book Bitches are stranded in the snow. Their inn lost power and didn't have a fireplace or a backup generator. They decided to make a run for town, but now they're stuck. Agnes thinks they might be closest to us."

"Damn it," I said, already across the room and into my bedroom to start layering up my clothes.

"The roads are closed. Help can't make it from town anytime soon." Maisie followed me into the room, worry on her face, the phone still in her hand.

"I'm going for them."

"Oh, you can't. The snowbanks are so high—"

Maisie's words cut off when I turned and gave her a look.

"Right. Okay. We're going after them."

"*We* are not. You are staying here. *I* am going." I pulled an extra sweater over my head.

"Agnes says the power is going out everywhere. The snow is too heavy on the powerlines. They're hoping to clear the roads enough to get everyone to the castle where there are backup generators. But it will just take time. Loren Brae is equipped for some snow, but nothing like this."

"Stoke the fire, get hot water boiling. I'm certain I saw a hot water bottle somewhere. Grab the blankets from the basket by the fire. I'm going to go to the shed and see if they have any sort of shovel."

"Good shout." Maisie had dressed beside me and right before she dashed off to do her tasks, I grabbed her hand and pulled her to me for a searing kiss.

"You're staying here."

"Like hell I am."

Rolling my eyes at her stubbornness, I layered two pairs of wool socks and bent to put my boots on.

"Did Agnes say how long they'd been out there?" Thankfully their phones still worked.

"An hour or so." Maisie called from the kitchen. "Found two hot water bottles."

"Great."

The lamp next to me flicked off and I looked up as Maisie swore from the kitchen.

"Power's gone."

"Then definitely keep the fire going." I wasn't sure if the cottage had a backup generator, but now wasn't the time to look for one. Striding to the front door, I peered out of the window. Snow gusted by, tossed about in the icy wind, and in any other circumstance I would think this looked like a picture-perfect postcard. Snow was beautiful until you had to deal with a blizzard's worth of it.

"I'm just going to the shed and then I'll be back." Opening the door quickly, I stepped out into the freezing air, snapping the door closed behind me to avoid too much heat escaping. Looking down, I groaned. Snow piled high against the cottage, making it almost impossible to see the faint outline of the two steps down to the ground. A tapping at the window had me turning to see Maisie brandishing a broom. Smart woman. She opened the door a crack and passed it through and I went about sweeping the steps. It was tedious work, as it wasn't the most effective tool against heavy wet snow, but soon enough I was able to see the steps and with the help of my makeshift shovel, I could navigate the short distance to the shed. Already, I'd worked up a light sweat under all of my layers, and I wondered how the Scots dealt with being both sweaty and freezing at the same time.

Luck was on my side because not only was the shed unlocked, but it also held a snow shovel. I considered a long bundle of climbing rope for a moment. Grabbing both, I trudged back to the cottage and leaned the shovel against the door before popping back inside.

Maisie stood at the door, coat on, a stubborn tilt to her chin.

"Maisie. You need to stay here. I can't be worried about you and the women too."

"You're not going alone. You don't even *have* snow where you are from."

"Nevertheless, it will be safer for you here."

"Tell me again why it's safe for you to wander alone into a whiteout?"

Damn it, but the woman had a point.

"So they only have one body to find instead of two?"

"Not funny." Maisie glared at me, and I sighed. Turning, I held up the rope.

"Listen, I have no idea how far away they are, but I feel like we could get lost quickly. Should we try tying this to the house? I mean, it might be silly—"

"Maybe, maybe not. Extra precautions never hurt. Let's go, West. I'm scared for them."

"I am too." I took the pack that Maisie had stuffed with blankets and hot water bottles and then waited while she tied the climbing rope to the front pillar of the little porch that covered the front door.

"Bloody hell," Maisie said as we turned to the snow. "It's both beautiful and terrifying, isn't it?"

A soft mooing sounded, and we both jumped as Clyde appeared, tiptoeing gently forward as though not to scare us. He tilted his big shaggy head, his eyes filled with concern.

"Is he—"

"Yeah, I think he's worried about us."

"Clyde." Maisie stepped forward and the ghost coo did a little jig on the top of the snow at the mention of his name. "Can you lead us to the Book Bitches? They're stranded in a car down the way."

The large ghost coo swung his head in the direction of the road, and my breath caught. For a moment, a glimmer of the proud coo he once had been shimmered through, his large head held high, his muscular body poised for action as the storm raged around him. Clyde huffed out a breath, bobbing his head, before walking slowly forward. When he stopped and glanced over his shoulder, I realized he was indeed leading us to the stranded car.

"We have to go slow. We have to shovel our way."

There was no way that I could properly shovel a path for us, what with some of the drifts being knee deep and higher, but at the very least, I could stop us from sinking too deeply into the snow. Bending to the task, we moved slowly forward, with Maisie unfurling the rope, and Clyde gently leading us through the storm. As we passed Maisie's truck, now almost totally buried due to the way the wind blew the snow straight from the loch, I glanced back at her.

"Looks like the truck's front end was already stuck in a snowbank."

"Does it?" Maisie wore an innocent expression. "How odd. It must be the way the snow is blowing."

Despite the seriousness of the situation, I laughed and bent my head to the task at hand as the wind picked up. We'd been smart to bring the rope, and I was grateful for Clyde, who steadfastly plodded along ahead of us. Because with the way the wind tore around us, it was almost impossible to see more than a few feet in front of me. The going was tedious, with me stopping every few minutes to catch my breath from shoveling, and to check that Maisie was hanging on. Worry for the Book Bitches pushed me forward though and I ignored my frozen jeans clinging to my legs as I continued on.

"Mooooo!" Clyde bellowed and I looked up to see the car, one side already covered in snow from where the gusts of snow piled.

"There it is!" I shouted and worked faster, nearing the car in no time.

"Clyde," Maisie called, and the coo pranced closer. "You're quite the hero. Thank you for bringing us here. Can you go for help? We want to get these women back to the cottage fast, but our power is out."

Clyde promptly winked from sight, and I had no idea what kind of help he could bring, but either way, the ghost coo was our hero today.

Four worried faces peered at me through the window when we arrived, and then smiles broke out on their faces. Opening the door a crack, Esther looked up at me.

"Took you long enough."

"This better not have been one of your hairbrained matchmaking schemes," I warned.

"While we do like drama, even this is too much for us. It was an unfortunate set of circumstances is all," Meredith promised over her shoulder.

"We have to get you out of the car, but the snow is quite deep. I think it's best if I carry you." I slid the backpack off my shoulders and widened the opening of the door to pass it inside to the women. "Blankets and hot water bottles. Wrap yourselves in the blankets. We'll go one by one."

"I can walk," Cherise said, and Shannon nodded in agreement.

"I'd like to say that I can, but I had surgery on my ankle not too long ago," Meredith admitted, giving me an apologetic look.

"I'm not going to pass up a chance to have a big, strong man carry me to safety," Esther said. "We all need a hero, don't we, darling?" Esther pitched her voice louder so Maisie could hear it from behind me and I rolled my eyes.

"Didn't we discuss you trying to be subtle?" I asked.

"Why bother? It's much more fun this way."

After a flurry of bickering and maneuvering, everyone was out of the car, wrapped in blankets, and I knelt in the snow so Meredith could climb onto my back.

"You're going to have to hold on as I can't keep you as secure as I'd like."

"Oh *no*," Meredith mock wailed. "I'll have to hold extra tightly to the big, strong man. Whatever am I going to do?"

These women were impossible. Leaning forward, I lifted Esther easily into my arms and she giggled.

"Och, now this is quite romantic, isn't it?"

"Stop your flirting and get on with it, Esther. It's a dreich day," Shannon shouted from behind me as the wind shook us.

"Worse than dreich, I'd say," Cherise said.

"A touch blustery," Meredith agreed.

"Nothing we can't handle, ladies. Should we sing Christmas songs?"

Honestly, I was fairly certain this entire group had lost their minds, but I had to admit, as their tremulous voices rose in a rousing song, I couldn't help but admire their spirit. Slowly, we trudged back to the cottage, every step a slog, as the wind battered us, and Maisie led the way with the rope. Sweat poured down my back beneath my sweater and my face had gone numb from the cold. I couldn't focus on anything other than one step in front of the other, as worry kicked up that I would slip and drop one of the women. They were a cumbersome package to carry, and I would kick myself if I hurt one of them trying to get them to safety.

"I see it," Maisie called, and the women cheered.

"Wait, were you both at the cottage together in the blizzard?" Esther exclaimed in excitement.

"Snowed in at the cottage," Meredith sighed at my ear. "It's my favorite trope."

CHAPTER THIRTEEN

Maisie

The fire had dwindled by the time we'd returned, but the cottage still held its warmth and we set to brushing the snow off the women, warming hands, and making sure everyone was safe.

West was simply amazing. He was not used to this bone-numbing cold, and yet he hadn't balked once at jumping into danger to help these women, who until recently, had been strangers to him. He'd shown himself to be both selfless and gallant. *It was hard not to fall for a man like this.* It wasn't surprising that my heart was pattering wildly as I looked at him. *He's amazing. How can I care so deeply for someone I barely know? Why does the thought of him leaving here, leaving me, make me feel desperately saddened?*

"There's nothing like being carried by a strapping lad through the snow." Esther lorded her adventure over the two who had walked behind West. Shaking my head, I bit

A KILT FOR CHRISTMAS

back a smile and picked up my phone to text Agnes. When the text didn't go through, I tried again, and then saw that the signal bars were empty in the corner.

"West," I hissed, motioning him closer. He walked over to me, a concerned look on his face.

"What's wrong?"

"Phones are out." I held up my phone, worry twisting in my stomach. Seeing my look, West wrapped his arms around me and pulled me close and I nestled in, needing him like I had needed my security blanket growing up.

"It'll be okay. There's plenty of firewood."

"Um, firewood won't fix this situation. There's no way to send an alert to call off the emergency rescue of the ladies, so someone else could be putting themselves in danger at the moment. I can't get in contact with Agnes to see if she made it to The Tipsy Thistle. I can't—"

"It's okay, love. I know. We have food and heat, so we're equipped on that front. Hopefully Agnes will trust that we got the Book Bitches back here safely and is wise to stay where she's safest. We're fine and—"

"Well, isn't this coorie?" Meredith beamed at us. Before I could respond, a bellow sounded from outside, causing us all to jump.

"What on earth?" Cherise said, and we all ran to the large windows at the front of the cottage.

The blizzard continued to rage, the midday light was murky, as the storm shrieked. Or was it the Kelpies? I'd heard tales of their spine-tingling screams in the night but had never been privy to the experience. Yet.

"What is that?" Shannon gasped.

"West! Look." I gripped West's arm as Clyde crested the

hill, pulling the sleigh that had been parked in front of MacAlpine Castle as part of their Christmas decorations. At the reins sat the tiniest man I'd ever seen, wrapped in a shearling jacket and a tiny red cap.

"Is that a wee child driving the sleigh?"

"Why can I see through the highland coo?"

"Is he singing?"

"What is happening?"

The Book Bitches' questions hammered us, and West looked down at me with a grin.

"I believe that Brice has made his entrance."

"Who is Brice?" Esther demanded.

"Ladies, welcome to Loren Brae. We've got a ghost coo and a kitchen broonie at your service. Not your traditional knights in shining armor, but we don't like to do things the usual way here."

A chorus of excitement rose from the women as I turned to the room and began to pack a bag. West snagged my arm.

"Are we really doing this?"

"I think we have to. They need us to get to the castle. Plus, do you want to spend however many days stuck in this cottage with these women?"

West's eyes widened and he grabbed a glass of water that had been sitting on the counter and strode over to the fireplace before tossing the contents on the flames. Using the poker to tamp the rest of the fire out, he called over his shoulder.

"Get ready for another cold trek, ladies. We're going to MacAlpine Castle."

"With the ghost coo?" Esther asked. "He looks a bit shoogly."

"He led us to your car to save you."

"And what a good ghost coo he is," Esther agreed, winding a blanket around her body again. Once we'd all put our coats back on and tucked blankets around us, I opened the door and peered outside where Clyde waited patiently, with Brice hunched over in the driver's seat. The wee broonie's body shook, and I realized even though he was magick, he still must be quite cold.

"Look at you, Clyde," I said, coming outside and infusing an admiring note into my voice. "Well done, sir. Well done. Thank you, Brice, for coming to our rescue."

Brice chattered something incomprehensible, his face buried in his scarf, and I could just see his eyes peering out at me beneath the hat he'd pulled low over his face.

"Right, ladies. On with it. Hurry, hurry. The wee lad is cold," I said, and ushered the women out into the snow. Standing by the sleigh, I helped Cherise and Shannon in, while West carried first Esther, and then Meredith, over to the sleigh. Once the four were settled, West handed me a pile of blankets and I climbed up and tucked them around the women. Turning, I looked at the remaining space on the seat. It would be a tight fit, but we had to make it work. West, seeing my concern, climbed into the sleigh.

"You should sit in the middle," Meredith said, nudging Esther over. "With Maisie on your lap. The weight needs to be distributed evenly."

The Book Bitches all readily agreed, moving so fast that it was clear they were on Team West. I wasn't going to argue with them, however, as it did make sense for West to sit in the middle. Once settled, he pulled me onto his lap, and I tucked a blanket around us. As I'd thought, it was a tight fit, but we were in.

"Do you think this thing will hold us?" I whispered to West.

"There's only one way to find out."

"Now, Dasher. Now, Dancer," Meredith cried out and Clyde was so excited that he leapt forward, the sleigh lurching behind him wildly. Brice shrieked, tugging on the reins, and corrected our course. I honestly couldn't believe it, but we were moving. No, perhaps I honestly couldn't believe that a *highland ghost coo* and a *broonie* were in charge of our passage. Our lives. It certainly wasn't the sleigh ride I'd anticipated.

But Clyde was *actually* doing it. He was pulling the sleigh like a Clydesdale, his shaggy mane rippling behind him in the wind, his large head jutting proudly into the air. My heart clenched. I knew without a shadow of a doubt that, for the rest of my life, I'd remember this moment as the sleigh barreled down the hill, driven by a broonie and propelled by a magnificent ghost coo, while the storm fought us.

West's arms tightened around my waist as we slid around a corner and out onto the road, which had yet to be cleared. Nerves skittered through me at the sight that greeted us. Easily two feet of snow blanketed the lane, and I wasn't surprised that emergency crews hadn't been able to make headway in this storm yet.

As we cruised toward Loren Brae, the sleigh jolting and jostling across the snow, my breath caught when the village came into view. I'd never seen the likes of it in my life. It was like someone had come along with a giant fire extinguisher and coated the entire town in foam. Except replace foam with snow. Snow was piled so high that I could barely make out the lumps that were cars parked on the side of the road, and the wind continued to slice across the icy dark water of the loch, which was just now starting to freeze.

"That's enough now," I surprised myself by yelling at the sky, and even Brice glanced over his shoulder at me. "Whatever is making this happen, it can stop now. We've had enough snow."

I wasn't sure what I thought would happen, that the storm would suddenly shut off like someone had flipped a switch, and when another gust of wind slapped me in the face, I wrinkled my nose in disgust.

"Do you think we need to go back to the stones to unwish the wish?" West asked at my ear.

"I have no idea. But it's not likely we'd even find it in this mess. Plus, we need to get these ladies into the warmth." Trying to find the standing stones was out of the question right now. Not only would it put us in unnecessary danger, but it would put those who might have to come help us in danger as well.

Clyde turned at the gates to the castle and rocketed up the drive, and we all screamed as the sleigh swung wildly. For a second, I was certain we were going to topple over but the sleigh managed to stay upright as we rounded the bend and the castle appeared.

Lachlan stood at the door, Sir Buster in his arms, and a look of relief crossed his face as the sleigh skidded to an admittedly shaky stop in front of him. Instantly, both Brice and Clyde disappeared, and we were left packed into the sleigh like sardines, smiling up at Lachlan. He gaped down at us, shaking his head, as Sir Buster bared his teeth in welcome.

"Never would I have thought I'd see the day ..." Lachlan said, trotting down the steps. Sir Buster, who was sporting a dashing wee Christmas sweater, pawed at him, and Lachlan put him down on a track that had been shoveled into the snow. Sir Buster raced through the track, taking a moment to relieve himself, before streaking back inside. If he'd had the strength, I was certain he would have slammed the door behind him.

"Ladies, welcome. And West, nice of you to join us." Lachlan held out a hand to Esther, ever the gentleman, even though the wind was still hitting us with its icy blasts.

"You'll need to carry me." Esther managed to both issue an order and flutter her lashes at Lachlan at the same time.

"Of course." In no time at all, Lachlan had retrieved both Meredith and Esther, carrying them neatly to the castle, while West helped me down. Then he turned and held his arms out to Cherise.

"Oh, I don't need—" Cherise started to wave his help away and then stopped. "Oh screw it. Why do they get to have all the fun?" She mimicked swooning, throwing a hand to her head, and dropped into West's outreached arms. He staggered a step back, but managed to stay standing, while I waited with Shannon.

"You as well?" I asked, smiling up at Shannon.

"I certainly can't be the only damsel in distress who doesn't get her knight now, can I?" Shannon pointed out. West returned and carried Shannon to the door, while I followed in his tracks. The wind was fierce at our backs, and

I couldn't help but worry that I'd really cursed the whole town. I needed to find Agnes and talk to her, because the guilt I was feeling over my wish right now was overwhelming.

"We've all set up camp in the restaurant, basically, as there are plenty of tables and chairs for everyone. Lia's cooking up a storm, the fires are on, and everyone seems to be in fairly good spirits. I'll warn you though, it's a bit chaotic. We've taken in those who lost power and didn't have backup at their home, which meant their pets came along as well. Sir Buster is having an absolute fit."

"I don't doubt it," I said.

"He tried to come with the sleigh. I had to go take him out of it. It's just too cold for the wee man to be out in the storm," Lachlan said.

"Will ... the broonie be okay? I saw he was shivering." I lowered my voice as we neared the kitchen, having followed Lachlan through a long stone hallway lined with old portraits.

"Brice will be fine. He'll be chattering away happily enough in the pantry and dreaming up his next way to be cheeky, I'm sure."

Lachlan wasn't wrong. We walked through the door to the restaurant and stepped into bedlam.

About half of the tables at Lia's restaurant were full, and the others had been pulled aside to clear space for children to run in careening circles in a play area. A few cats prowled the edges of the room while a pack of dogs were currently in a stand-off with Sir Buster, who looked ever the leader in his fuzzy wee sweater. Lady Lola, sensing trouble, strolled unconcerned between the pack that faced Sir

Buster, gave him a lick to the side of the head, and instantly the tension dissolved, and the dogs got down to the business of playing.

My eyes followed West as he found Matthew and they embraced as longtime friends do, and Lachlan followed my look.

"He's class. You could do far worse, Maisie."

"Who are we talking about?" Agnes said at my shoulder, and I spun to give her a relieved hug.

"I'm so glad we made it. A freakin' ghost coo drove us on a sleigh," I hissed under my breath and Agnes grinned at me.

"Och, I've been telling you for ages, Maisie. Loren Brae has magick on so many levels."

"But I never knew it was like *this*." I threw my hand out in the air, almost knocking a tray from Lia's hands as she passed, but she neatly dodged my awkward flailing. "There are ghosts and wee kitchen elves and ... so, all this time and all of these rumors ... are the Kelpies actually real?"

Agnes grabbed my arm and pulled me back into the kitchen, away from the bedlam of the restaurant, and I smiled at an older woman humming as she pulled a tray of scones from the oven. The scent had my mouth watering.

"Yes, Maisie. The Kelpies are *actually* threatening Loren Brae. It's what I've been working on so hard. We're trying to restore the Order of Caledonia. If we do, well, the stone of truth will be protected, and the Kelpies will go dormant once more. Until then, they can show at any time."

"I thought I heard them shrieking in the night. But it was hard to tell, the wind was so high." I had so many questions about the magickal Order of Caledonia, but with the amount of people bustling in and out of the kitchen, I realized it would have to wait. I had more pressing concerns to deal with. "Listen ... I, well, I think this is all my fault."

Agnes looked over her shoulder and then bent her head closer to mine.

"What, specifically, is your fault?"

"This. The storm."

Agnes looked like she wanted to laugh but then sobered when she saw my stricken expression.

"Why do you say that?"

"At the stones? The other night? I'd just come from the pub. I hadn't thought much about it, but winning the sleigh ride was in my head. I didn't, well, I didn't really believe in the whole Christmas Wish thing, so I just made an offhand, throwaway wish."

"You wished for snow, didn't you?" Agnes's eyes widened.

"The snowiest Christmas ever. To be exact."

"Shite," Agnes cursed and Lia skidded to a stop next to her. The chef had her hair tied back with a bandana and a healthy pink flush on her cheeks.

"What's up?" Lia's American accent cut through our conversation.

"Maisie wished for the snowiest Christmas ever at the standing stones. What spell do you have to counteract that?"

Lia nodded, not the least bit fazed about Agnes asking her for a spell, and crossed the room to take a leatherbound book out of a basket on top of a spice cabinet. She pursed her lips as she paged through it, and I gaped at her.

"Spell?" I asked weakly.

"Yup. Lia's a kitchen witch. She's the second member of the Order of Caledonia. Sophie's the first. She's the knight."

I blinked at Agnes like she'd lost her mind, but before I could ask more questions—because trust me, I had a million of them—Lia came to my side.

"Here's one that might work. It's like a reverse 'no takesies backsies.' Basically, you have to state your intent for whatever you've manifested to be revoked." Lia looked up at me.

"I kind of did that already. Like, outside. In the sky. Just shouted it."

"That's a start, but let me brew you a quick tea and we'll just have ourselves a little ritual, shall we? Can't hurt, right?"

"Scone?" The older woman appeared at my side with a basket of cheddar and spring onion scones, and I took one along with the napkin she offered. It was piping hot and crumbly in my mouth, and I chewed it absentmindedly while I watched Lia mutter to herself at her spice chest.

"Kitchen witch, huh?"

"We're basically just a magickal wee town full of surprises," Agnes said.

"I can't believe you didn't tell me all of this."

"I have been telling you. For years. You just always brushed it off."

I thought back to all the times Agnes had brought up the Kelpies, the history of MacAlpine Castle, or had spoken about the Stone of Truth. I'd never much paid serious attention to her ramblings, as she was always talking about some book or another, and now I realized that all this time it hadn't been fictional plots of stories she'd been reading. She'd been trying to tell me, in her own way, that Loren Brae was, essentially, enchanted.

And it had taken a ghost coo to basically run me over before I'd finally listened.

"I'm a freaking eejit." I sighed. Shame mixed with excitement in my stomach. I felt bad for ignoring Agnes for so long, but also, how cool was this? It was like I had a whole new town to explore, and even though I couldn't afford to go on vacation, now I could explore a new magickal world.

"You are. But you're my favorite eejit." Agnes kissed me on the cheek, and we drew closer to the worktable when Lia gestured us over. Picking up the kettle, she poured steaming water into a cup and stirred the contents three times in a counterclockwise motion.

"Give that a moment to cool and we'll crack on with the ritual," Lia said.

"You've got quite a party going on in there tonight, will you be able to feed them all?" Agnes asked Lia as we waited. Lia grinned, never stopping moving, as she chopped garlic at her cutting board.

"Never ask a chef if she's capable of feeding everyone." Lia's knife whirred, making neat slices, as she slid the cut pieces into a bowl. "I'm going back to my roots. Italian comfort food. It's easy to make big portions, and nobody turns their nose up at my mama's red sauce."

"Smart. Honestly, everything you make is mouthwateringly good. We lucked out getting you here," Agnes said.

"I agree. I know I've only been here to eat once, but it was to die for," I added.

"Thank you, ladies. I have to say, I really think I've finally found my home. It feels good." Lia's cheeks warmed, and I couldn't help but notice the pretty emerald engagement ring on her finger. "Tea should be ready now."

Lia put down the knife and handed me the cup, a gentle smile on her face.

"Think about what you said at the standing stones and then repeat after me."

"*Words spoken in haste.*
Must be replaced,
With that I take back my intent,
All shall be well in this moment."

I repeated her words and then drank the tea as instructed. When I was finished, I looked up and waited.

"That's it. Nothing else we can do but ride it out."

"Here's hoping. Thanks, Lia."

"Hey, ladies! Get your cute bums in here." Graham stuck his head in the kitchen and winked at us as Agnes rolled her eyes. "Karaoke's on."

"Oh, we can't miss this."

We walked into the restaurant just in time to see West and Matthew, back-to-back, microphones in hand, with the Book Bitches as their backup dancers. West caught my eye and with a wide smile, he pointed at me and sang off-key.

"All I want for Christmas is mooooooo!"

My heart melted as fast as a snowball in front of a fire and Agnes gave me side-eye.

"You're a goner, aren't you?"

"Oh yeah, well and truly done. This man has my heart."

CHAPTER FOURTEEN

Maisie

It had been four blissful days since the storm of the century, and it was all anyone could talk about in Loren Brae. Tonight was Christmas Eve, and I was taking extra time to get ready at Agnes's flat, before going to the party that Graham was hosting at The Tipsy Thistle.

I still wasn't sure if it was the ritual or if the storm had just run its course, but either way, a few hours after we'd done the ritual, the snow had stopped as abruptly as it had arrived. Perhaps the storm had gotten fed up with our terrible karaoke songs. Luckily, on the back end of the storm had been a warm front—well as warm as it ever got in Scotland—and a large chunk of the snow had melted, leaving it easier to clear the roads and get on with life. Agnes had decided to postpone the book festival until the new year, so I'd spent the last few days largely with West.

And what a few days it had been.

We'd taken walks in the snow, albeit not as long as I

would have liked because *somebody* still hadn't acclimated to the cold weather in Scotland. But I still loved the fact that he was willing to give it a go, with minimal complaints, and I always rewarded him handsomely when we returned to the cottage. We talked about books, our jobs, our friends, and just any little thing really. West was open-minded, easy-going, and I loved listening to him talk about the things that got him excited. He had an incredible lecturer's voice, and when he got started on a subject that interested him, well, let's just say that I could fully understand why that undergrad had shown up naked in his office at work.

Needless to say, I was head over heels.

And frankly, terrified. I knew he had a plane ticket home soon, but every time he'd tried to talk to me about it, I'd shut him down or changed the subject. Maybe I just needed to live in this bubble of happiness for a while longer before I had to accept the reality that our lives were worlds apart. It didn't help that he'd already told me that his last long-distance relationship hadn't worked for him. Where would that leave us? And she had been a famous freaking rock star. If he couldn't make it work with her, I wasn't sure I was ready to accept what that would mean for us. So I carried on, pushing reality away for another day, and just enjoyed the time that I did have with West. If that was all I ever got, I would hold every moment to my heart like a carefully wrapped Christmas gift.

"Are you ready?" Agnes called and I joined her in the living room.

"You look cute," we both said at the same time. Agnes wore a deep green sweater and fitted leather pants, and I had on my bright red sweater and a Santa hat. I'd swiped on some eye makeup and used a touch of lipstick.

I was looking forward to giving West his gift. I'd found him a vintage edition book of Robert Burns' poems, knowing that he would enjoy Scotland's favorite poet.

Together we raced down the stairs, giggling like schoolgirls when the cold air hit our face. Agnes threaded her arm through mine, and we paused to look at the shimmering reflection of Loren Brae on Loch Mirren's dark surface.

"Is Loren Brae going to be okay?" I asked, worry slipping through me. I still had a lot to learn about this magickal Order that Agnes was trying to put to rights, but I'd been so involved with West that I hadn't had much time to talk to Agnes about it.

"Likely so. We'll do our best." Agnes squeezed my arm. "But that's a worry for another day."

The party was already in full swing when we walked into The Tipsy Thistle. The Book Bitches were clustered around the bar, openly flirting with Graham, who also wore a Santa hat and a simple, fitted long-sleeved black shirt. He looked knock-out handsome, and I slid a glance at Agnes, but her attention was elsewhere. Or she was purposely ignoring him. It was hard to tell with those two.

West, Lachlan, Munroe, and Matthew all sat at the bar, and Lottie, Archie, and Hilda played cards at a table and chatted happily. I immediately wanted to go join their card game but had to force down my competitive streak and veered toward the bar. Along one wall, a long table had been set up and there were plates of shortbread, various desserts, and several crockpots full of food. Graham had indicated everyone who felt like bringing a dish should, and

Agnes and I had baked a fruit loaf earlier today. A fire crackled in the fireplace, Christmas music played merrily in the background, and the scent of cinnamon and nutmeg filled the air. All was perfect in my world. Though I'd never been a huge fan of Christmas one way or the other, I realized how nice it was to be here, surrounded by people I actually enjoyed and cared about.

"You may just be the best Christmas gift I've ever received." West materialized in front of me, and I grinned shyly up at him. He wore a grey thick wool sweater, which frankly, I'd be roasting in if I was wearing it, and a headband with antlers on it. A lovely thread of longing unfurled inside of me. It made me both wistful and excited, this knowing I held for him, and I wished I had all the answers now.

"Merry Christmas," I began, and paused when he leaned down and kissed me.

We hadn't talked much about our relationship or the future—largely due to me wanting to stay in the moment—and now my heart skipped a beat as he claimed me in front of the entire pub. Voices stilled around us for a moment and then the chatter picked up again. It was so typical of a small town. They took notice, made a note for their morning gossip, and continued their conversations. When he pulled away, a giddy bubble of excitement built in me.

"You look great. That hat looks cute on you." West flicked the end of my hat.

"Thank you. Nice horns."

"I certainly can't compete with Clyde, but I'll do my best."

"Is this where I insert a joke about giving me a ride?" I

winked at West and was rewarded when his cheeks flushed. I had already found that I did, indeed, enjoy unbuttoning this very buttoned-up man. He was so very precise and polite in his day-to-day interactions that it had been an absolute surprise to discover how he took charge in the bedroom. Even now, surrounded by all these people, I couldn't help but think about sneaking away to the cottage with him the moment we could get away.

"Let me get you a drink before I take you up on that look in your eyes." West guided me to the bar where Agnes scowled at Graham.

"It doesn't count." Agnes crossed her arms over her chest.

"I believe the rules of mistletoe are clear," Graham said, and I laughed when I saw he'd changed out his Santa hat for a headband that hung a sprig of mistletoe over his forehead.

"It's only if you happen upon mistletoe. Like, by happenstance. By chance. Not because someone forces it in your face," Agnes said.

"Don't you want to unwrap your gift, Agnes?" Graham winked and leaned closer to her.

"If you're my gift then I must have been very naughty this year," Agnes scoffed.

"A side of you I'd dearly love to explore more."

Graham laughed when Agnes muttered something under her breath and slid a package across the bar. Agnes glared at it suspiciously.

"What is this?"

"Your Christmas gift, darling."

"You didn't have to get me anything."

"I'm well aware, but nevertheless, here it is." Graham

took his mistletoe headband off and put his Santa hat back on before turning to me. "A drink for you tonight? We've got a lovely spiced egg nog if you fancy it."

"Perfect, thank you." I bumped shoulders with Agnes as she poked at the ribbon on the package. "Are you going to open that?"

"Why did he have to go and get me a gift? We never do gifts."

"Maybe the pub has had a good year."

"It hasn't. Not with the Kelpies scaring everyone off." Agnes worried her lower lip as Graham returned with my drink.

"It's not going to blow up," Graham promised, his grin widening at Agnes's mulish look.

"We never do gifts," Agnes said, raising her eyes to Graham's.

"Things can change, can't they?"

I bit back a smile as Agnes huffed, clearly in distress, and waited while she carefully pulled back the paper to show a small velvet jewelry box. My heart danced as Agnes's expression turned downright sour.

"How long have these two been at it?" West whispered in my ear.

"As long as I've known them. They grew up together. I think they even dated lightly way back in the day, but it didn't take."

"There's always an option for a second chance, right?"

"I think so." I watched as Agnes gingerly opened the lid to reveal a delicate silver necklace with a small book charm. Agnes's mouth rounded and she picked it up to read the inscription on the charm.

"Bonnie Books." A wide smile bloomed on Agnes's face, and she jumped up, leaned over the counter, and brushed her lips across Graham's cheek. For a moment, his eyes closed, as though he wanted to savor the kiss, and then Agnes popped back down onto her stool and clapped her hands. "This is surprisingly sweet of you, Graham. I love it. Truly."

"Just keeping you on your toes, darling. I've got to start wooing you now if I'm expecting to marry you at sixty. It'll likely take me a few decades to convince you."

"What's this now?" I laughed at Agnes's stricken expression.

"I told him that I'd marry him if I hadn't married by the time I was sixty. It was an offhand comment that apparently, he's taking to heart."

"A promise is a promise," Graham said, whistling a cheerful tune as he went to serve a group of people who had crowded through the door.

"That man drives me crazy." Agnes rolled her eyes. Still, she quickly put her necklace on, and I leaned over to admire it against her sweater.

"It's really pretty. He did a good job."

"Yes, yes, enough about Graham and how amazing he is," Agnes griped. We all jumped as Hilda rang a handbell from across the room. At her signal, Graham turned the music low, and the pub quieted.

"We wanted to wish everyone a very Merry Christmas after a harrowing few days with the storm." Everyone clapped. "We can't tell you how happy we all are that nobody was seriously injured, and I have to say, I think we're going to start a new tradition of Karaoke Christmas at the castle." Cheers erupted and I couldn't help but laugh. We'd had a ton of fun that night, and I could only imagine how great it would be through the years as the tradition took hold. Lachlan came to stand by Hilda, a large box in his hands.

"We also wanted to give a special welcome and a thank-you to our guest, Weston Smith, for his heroic efforts in rescuing the famous Book Bitches of Kingsbarns from their trapped car."

"World-famous," Esther piped in.

"You didn't have to do anything for—"

"Come on up. It's the least Loren Brae could do for stepping in to help when we needed you."

"West! West! West!" The pub started chanting West's name and I laughed as he went up and took the package from Lachlan.

"Go on, open it, lad!"

Putting the gift on the table, West opened the box and removed the tissue, surprise crossing his face. Reaching in, he pulled out a heavy wool kilt in a tartan pattern of green, red, and grey. The pub cheered once more as he held it up to himself, a bewildered smile on his face.

"This is incredible," West said. Turning, he hugged Lachlan, and then Hilda, thanking them profusely.

"Every good lad deserves a kilt for Christmas," Archie said from where he sat, shaking West's hand.

"My own honorary kilt." West beamed.

"You're one of us now, lad. And welcome anytime." Lachlan clapped him on the back, and the pub cheered once more as West came back to my side, with a delighted grin.

"I, for one, can't wait to see you in it."

"That can certainly be arranged," West said, putting the gift at the end of the bar so it was out of the way. "That was really nice of everyone. I've always secretly wanted a kilt."

"It's even better when it's given to you. Now it will have more meaning."

The Book Bitches surrounded us, and I took a moment to carefully survey their respective Christmas shirts. It was Esther's shirt that made me pause.

"How did you make that so fast?" I demanded.

"Cri-cut machine."

"You brought it with you?"

"Sure did."

Her shirt had a sleigh being pulled by a coo and the words read, *Sleigh All Day*.

"I'm going to need one of those," I decided.

"Oh, I already planned for it. But it'll be a bit as I need to get back to my craft room for more supplies. I'll mail you one once I have it made up. I'm so glad you finally came to your senses."

"What's that now?" I blinked down at the older woman who smiled cheerfully up at me.

"We've been trying to get you and West together. I'm glad to see it."

"With all of the subtlety of a nuclear explosion," West chimed in, overhearing her words.

"Bah. We didn't kidnap her, did we? It was just luck that had her snowed in with you."

"Kidnap?" I raised an eyebrow at West, and he shook his head at me, a pained expression on his face.

"Don't ask."

The night passed quickly, as drinks flowed, food was restocked, and Christmas memories were shared around the fire. It was close to midnight when people finally started packing up and West grabbed my arm.

"I've been meaning to give you your gift all night—"

"Oh, let me get yours." I dug in my handbag, also having forgotten. He paused what he was saying and then took the slim package from me. "Go on, open it."

I waited while he carefully opened the package and was rewarded when delight flooded his face. Holding the book up, he smiled at me, before leaning over to brush a soft kiss over my lips.

"This is really beautiful, Maisie. Thank you. I'll treasure it always."

"Good, I'm glad. I didn't want to get anything big, well, what with your travel and all, but found this in Bonnie Books and it just—"

"It's truly great. I love it." West tapped my nose to get me to stop rambling and then handed me an envelope. "And here is my gift that I am so excited to give you. Merry Christmas, Maisie."

"You didn't have to—"

"Just open it," West ordered. I complied and pulled out a folded piece of paper. Opening it, I realized it was an email that had been printed out. I read the words out loud.

"'West, great to hear from you. On your recommendation, I read Maisie's manuscript and loved it. I would be happy to represent her if she'd be open to talking contract specifics. We can chat in the new year if you'll connect us? Hope you have a great Christmas! Cheers! John.'" I blinked up at West in confusion, as icy panic gripped me. "What is this?"

"Maisie. I read your book. It's wonderful, truly, it is. John Batemen is a great literary agent, so I passed it over to him to see if he'd be interested, and it appears he is. Isn't that great?"

West beamed at me, so excited to give me this gift, as my world crashed around me. Getting up, I grabbed my purse and ran outside without saying goodbye to anyone, tears flooding my eyes. I didn't know what to do, or think, just that I had to get out of there. I needed space to breathe. This was all too much.

"Maisie! Wait. Wait." West caught up with me, pulling me around the corner of the pub and away from the curious eyes of a few people who were leaving the party. Our breath fogged in the cool night air and West took off his glasses to wipe them before putting them back on his nose. "I'm sorry. Was that the wrong thing to do?"

"Yes!" I shouted. Whirling, I clutched the email. "No. Yes. I don't know."

"Please, can you tell me what's wrong? I want to understand why you're upset."

As did I.

Panic warred with excitement in my gut, and finally fear rose up, clenching my heart as I turned to look at him. This perfect man, standing in the light of the streetlamp, waiting patiently for me to explain my insecurities. He offered an escape to a world I was entirely unsure of, with palm trees and famous singers, literary agents and sandy beaches, while I was just a failed writer who worked at the local post office. Who would I be in West's world? Would I even fit? It sounded so exotic, so daunting, that I was certain I might just turn tail and run. And what would that do to West then? I'd break his heart if he rearranged his future for me and I couldn't hack it.

"It's just that ... I don't need your favors, West. I don't need someone to come in and help poor wee Maisie from a small town get her first break. I can do it on my own, you ken?" I slipped into a bit of Scottish as I began to pace. "This was my dream. Mine. I needed to do it by myself."

"But you *did* do it, Maisie. I *loved* the book. I never would have passed it on to John if I hadn't loved it. And trust me, agents are about making money. He wouldn't have minced words if he hadn't liked it."

"And if he hadn't liked it? Then what? Would you have told me?"

"I..." West shook his head, his shoulders slumping. "No, likely not."

"So you would have let me figure it out on my own, rejection after rejection, but now you can be the hero when you do get me a contract?" I knew that I was twisting things in my head, working myself up, but there was something far deeper at play here that forced me to do so. *Him giving the agent my manuscript was just an excuse to push him away.* Even in the throes of my angst, I could see that.

It wasn't about the manuscript.

I'd never really allowed myself to dream for more than what I'd had. The one time I had, was when I'd written my book and worked up the courage to send it off to agents. Over and over, with every rejection that I'd received, I'd been told not to dream. Now, West was handing me a dream future on a platter, and I couldn't help but feel like maybe the universe had been right all along. Maybe it was best to stay in my lane, surrounded by the familiar, never wishing for more. *Because that way led to heartbreak.* I couldn't quite trust myself to grab the future that West offered, or even understand if I deserved it, so I needed to push this good man away now before I well and truly failed him later on. I knew, as certain as I knew the sun rose in the east, that I would never meet a man like West again. The thought of potentially losing him down the road, when I was even more invested than I was now, was shaking me to my very core.

"I don't know. Maybe. Maybe not? Since I love the book, I would have probably kept encouraging you to write more and see what other contacts I had to help. I can't really say, Maisie. I just, I believe in you, and I believe in your book. I wanted to help."

"Kept encouraging me." I nodded and then looked up at him. "What are we doing here, West? What is all of this? You're hopping on a plane—"

"Tomorrow."

"Tomorrow? On Christmas day?" I stopped, panic gripping me.

"My mother fell. She'll need some help, so I'm going home early. I didn't want to ruin the night."

"I'm sorry to hear that," I said, stiffly, crossing my arms over my chest, as West came to me and put his hands on my shoulders.

"Maisie. Look at me." I lifted eyes filled with tears to him. "Tell me what's going on."

"We can't do this. Any of this. Our lives are worlds apart. It'll never work."

"So this isn't about the manuscript?"

"It's that too! I don't know," I said, blinking back the tears. "CeeCee freaking Rhodes couldn't even keep your love. A long-distance relationship made you guys fall apart. I'm no famous rock star, West. If you can't make it work with her, then how are you going to make it work with someone like me?"

"Someone like you?" West tilted his head, a dangerous note in his voice. "A brilliant, beautiful, full-hearted woman who makes me light up inside? The woman of my dreams, of my heart, the one that has filled me with so much love that I can't even see straight?"

"I don't know if I see myself the way you see me."

"Clearly not, or you'd give us, and your manuscript, the chance it deserves. I've had a lot of thoughts about you, Maisie, but I've never once thought you were a coward." West captured my chin in his hands and gave me a searing kiss before turning and walking away. By the time I'd gathered myself to go after him, the street was empty. *What just happened?* How did such a wondrous night, full of hope and joy, turn into ... this? *Heartbreak.*

West's words bounced around and around in my head.

"Clearly not, or you'd give us, and your manuscript, the chance it deserves. I've had a lot of thoughts about you, Maisie, but I've never once thought you were a coward."

Was I a coward? Surely trying over thirty times to submit my heart to publishers wasn't cowardice. But the words he said about me? *Brilliant, beautiful, full-hearted, love* ... Did I just reject something precious? A man so full of joy, intelligence, passion, and love?

I wasn't sure if I liked this side of myself and was almost

certain that one of my pep talks in the mirror wasn't going to fix this. West was right to walk away from me.

Agnes found me as my tears overflowed. "Come on then, let's get you upstairs. We'll get a cup of tea on and sort this all out. I promise."

"I don't think this one can be sorted," I sobbed.

"Nonsense. Even if it's a Christmas miracle, we can figure it out."

CHAPTER FIFTEEN

West

For once, I didn't mind the cold.

The sharp bite of the icy wind against my skin reminded me that I could still feel, even though I'd gone numb when Maisie had flip-flopped on me. My thoughts tangled around each other, trying to figure out where such a warm evening had gone wrong, and hating that I had to leave the next day. It all felt so unfinished, and messy, and the last thing I'd come to Scotland for was more drama.

"West! Hey, wait up." I turned to see Matthew on the street behind me, lugging the box with my gifted kilt inside of it. I'd totally forgotten about the gift. Not to mention paying for my bar tab.

"Shit, thanks. I need to go back and pay."

"No worries, man. I got it. I stepped outside on the tail end of the argument you were having and figured you wouldn't be coming back in. You okay?" Matthew asked as we turned where the street curved past the loch. Snow still drifted softly down, caught in the soft streetlights, and the dark waters shifted. Movement across Loch Mirren caught my eye, but I couldn't quite make out what it was.

"I don't think so, to be perfectly honest."

"Fair enough. A dram by the fire is called for. Let's—"

An otherworldly shriek split the night, and Matthew crushed the box to his chest, leaping behind me as my gut twisted.

"What the—"

"The Kelpies. Go, go, go," Matthew hissed, and I needed no further warning. We turned from the loch, our feet slipping on the packed snow, as we scrambled up the road away from the shoreline, racing toward the safety of the castle. From what I understood from myths and legends, Kelpies were murderous water horses, but I wasn't certain if that meant their power extended to land or not.

I also wasn't keen on finding out the answer to that particular question.

My breath puffed out in front of me in sharp bursts, and fear caused the hairs on the back of my neck to stand up as we skirted the top of the hill and neared the castle doors. Ghost coos and so-ugly-they're-cute broonies were one thing, but this felt like an entirely different ball game. I wasn't sure I wanted to play.

The doors opened before we arrived and Sophie stormed out, a sword in her hand and Lachlan at her back. I didn't know what was about to happen, but by the fierce look of determination in her eyes, I also didn't want to get in her way.

"Get inside, lads," Lachlan ordered, and I was more than happy to comply. While I wasn't one to leave a friend hanging in a fight, I also realized this was not my fight. I'd likely be more of a hindrance than a help, so I skidded through the doors and caught Sir Buster on the fly as he made an attempt to race outside.

"Not for you, buddy." Sir Buster growled, but when another shriek split the night, he instantly stopped and burrowed into my arms.

"Should we ..." I trailed off, panting, as Matthew and I came to a stop in the hallway. Our chests heaved with exertion and fear, and he held a hand up as he gulped air, my kilt box crumpled at his side.

"No. They ... it's a whole thing. The Order of Caledonia will handle it."

Now that was something I dearly wanted to unpack. Already fear was receding and being replaced by intrigue. *I mean, come on.* This was every literature professor's dream come true. *Hauntings and myths come to life?* There was no way I was going to leave Loren Brae now, at least not for long. Already I could see a million book ideas springing to life in my head, and how diving into research here would be exciting beyond words. Maybe it was stupid to be this excited about Kelpies, but once the initial threat had subsided, I wanted to race back outside to see if I could catch a glimpse of them.

"I have so many questions."

"I don't blame you. Shall we have that dram?" Matthew stamped snow off his boots, and I followed suit.

"You sure they'll be okay?" I asked when Matthew motioned for me to follow him to the library.

"Sophie's the only one who can hold them back. They're used to it by now, albeit a bit tired."

"Again, so many questions."

"And I have answers. First, tell me what happened." Matthew pushed open the door to a room I hadn't been in yet and my professor's heart gave a sigh of approval. We entered a massive library with a fire roaring in a rustic stone fireplace, a cozy window seat tucked next to it, and a pretty painted mural on the ceiling. Bookshelves lined the walls, with a rolling ladder to get to the top shelves, and intricate patterned rugs were tossed across the worn wood floors. I made my way to a leather lounge chair by the fire and dropped into it, helping Sir Buster to the floor when he growled at me. The dog plodded over to a tiny tartan bed by the fire, offering a huff of disapproval, before curling up in a tiny ball. I wondered if Lady Lola was about or if she'd found her sleep elsewhere.

"Here." Matthew handed me a dram of whisky and saluted me. "Sláinte."

I drank, the warmth of whisky heating my body, the smokiness lingering on my tongue.

"She ended it. Just up and ended it." One of my favorite things about my friend was his ability to be a good sounding board, and he listened without interruption until I finished the story.

"She's scared," Matthew summed up neatly when I finished speaking.

"Clearly." I sighed, taking another sip of the whisky, staring into the flames that tumbled over each other in the fireplace. "And I get that. This has all moved so fast. Maybe I shouldn't have given that manuscript to John. I thought I was helping."

"Maybe not. But even so, is that enough to end a relationship over? Mea culpa and all that, and then you get back to being together. No, this feels like something so much more." Matthew pursed his lips as he thought it over. Glancing up, he considered me. "What do *you* want?"

"Me? I want to be with her," I said automatically.

"Then why did you walk away?"

Ouch. The man had a point. But Maisie wasn't the only one with demons. I completely understood why CeeCee and I broke up, but it didn't mean my self-esteem hadn't taken a massive blow. *She had chosen her career over us, after all.* Yeah, that had stung.

"I guess I just wanted someone to choose me for once." It was embarrassing to have to admit that to my friend, and I kept my eyes trained on the fire to avoid any sympathetic looks from Matthew.

"That's understandable. Given what happened with CeeCee. So how are you going to play it?"

"I think I need to give her some time. And myself, really. It doesn't feel great to be rejected on Christmas Eve." I rubbed my hand across my chest.

"Yes, not ideal." *That was Matthew, ever succinct.* "You leave tomorrow?"

"Yeah, late. Overnight back home."

"There's time yet."

"I just need to figure out what she's so scared of." *There had to be time. Maisie was the woman I wanted to spend the rest of my life with. There was no other option.*

"Probably tying herself to that ugly face of yours," Matthew said, and despite everything, I laughed.

"How's that sex life of yours again, Matthew?"

"Bite me."

CHAPTER SIXTEEN

Maisie

I'd finally gone to bed well past three in the morning after crying it out with Agnes and then spent another hour in bed staring at the ceiling, coming to realize some hard truths about myself. By the time morning arrived, I'd only had a few hours of fitful sleep, but I was so worried that I would miss seeing West before he left that I was afraid to really let myself sleep.

After I showered and did my best to cover the dark circles under my eyes, I stared at myself in the mirror and gave myself one of my pep talks.

"If you can believe in a ghost coo and a broonie, you can damn well believe in yourself."

I mean, it wasn't my best pep talk, but it would have to do. Grabbing my handbag and phone, I flew out of the flat, knowing Agnes was likely still sleeping, and hopped in my truck that we'd retrieved from the snowbank at West's cottage. The morning was crisp and clear, with enough snow still hanging on to give Loren Brae a proper white Christmas, and cheerful puffs of smoke wound from chimneys around town. My heart hammered in my chest as I drummed my fingers on the steering wheel, trying to keep my speed in check as I drove to West's cottage.

My insecurities had gotten the better of me last night and I'd let a good man go home alone on Christmas Eve. It wasn't my best moment, and I prayed West would be willing to forgive me for not understanding all of the emotions that had thrown me into a tailspin.

Agnes had been a warrior last night. Every excuse I'd given her about why West and I wouldn't work, she'd shot down, and then she'd all but kicked my sorry arse across the room when I'd told her my reaction to the manuscript. Her lecture had been followed by a hug, two pieces of shortbread, and a cup of tea.

Pulling up at the cottage, I barely stopped the truck before I was out and racing to the front door. Pounding, I waited, my nerves kicking a staccato beat in my stomach. When nobody answered, I knocked again, peering through the window. Again, nothing. Turning, I walked down the steps and snuck to the bedroom window where the curtains were open, and my heart dropped.

The bed was neatly made.

It was then that I realized the cottage was totally empty. His luggage was gone, there were no dishes on the counter, and none of the lights were on. He'd already left.

I'd missed him.

And I'd likely missed my chance to win him back.

Tears welled and I grabbed my phone, calling Agnes as I sat in the front seat of my truck, furious with myself.

"What? Who, huh?" Agnes mumbled into the phone.

"He's gone. West is gone."

"He is?"

"Yes! His cottage is empty. Nobody's here. He's left. I screwed up." I cried openly now, my stomach twisted in knots.

"Wait, stop, hold on. Did you say the cottage?" Agnes started to sound more awake.

"Yes, his cottage. It's empty."

"He moved to the castle yesterday because he had to go home early and the cottage got a new booking for today over Hogmanay."

"What?" I said, hope blooming.

"He's at the castle. Or he should be. Lachlan's taking him to the airport this afternoon."

"Oh my God. I still have a chance."

"Go get 'em, lass." Agnes clicked off, likely annoyed that I'd woken her. Shifting the truck into gear, I raced to the castle with my heart in my throat. By the time I'd made it up the long drive, my heart was hammering in my chest, and a drop of sweat slipped down my spine beneath my jumper. When the castle finally appeared, I was treated to a picturesque Christmas scene that I hated having to interrupt.

A major Christmas morning snowball fight was in effect.

Everyone from the castle raced across the yard, ducking behind decorations and firing off shots when they could. Sir Buster, in a bright Christmas sweater, and Lady Lola, in a green tartan vest, barked and raced down their shoveled paths in the snow. Gingerly, I parked the truck and got out, my heart leaping when I spied West crouched behind a bush in the far corner.

He hadn't left yet.

"West!" I cried, starting forward.

A massive snowball hit me in the back, splattering against my shoulders, icy cold slush slapping my hair. Whirling, I glared to where Matthew stood, grinning, tossing another snowball between his hands.

"That's for hurting my friend."

"What the hell, Matthew! I'm here to make it right," I shouted.

Matthew shrugged.

"Better run then."

On a squeal, I turned to run toward West and was stopped short by a snowball to my face. I gasped, not because it hurt, but because the cold was such a shock to my system. Stunned, I wiped snow from my face as Matthew howled with laughter behind me. Blinking, I looked up and saw West grinning in front of me, another snowball in hand.

"You can't be serious." Here I was ready to pour my heart out to this man and he had just pummeled me in the face with a snowball.

"All's fair in love and war, doll," West said, and even though he was joking, I could see the flash of pain in his eyes.

"Oh, you're on." Reaching down, I went to pack a snowball and gasped as the men attacked. Retreat was my only option. Shrieking, I threw up my hands and ran behind a wall of the manicured garden, hoping to escape for a moment to build my arsenal. Footsteps pounded in the snow behind me, and I turned to see West hot on my heels. Distracted, my foot caught, and I went flying headfirst into a snowbank, my humiliation complete.

Really, why had I even bothered doing my makeup this morning?

West's hands dug into my hips, and he yanked, pulling me out of the snowbank so I sprawled backwards in the snow, gasping for air. He crouched over me, amusement dancing in his eyes, and waited while I caught my breath.

"Was it me you were coming to see this morning?" West finally asked.

"Of course it was, you eejit." Right, probably not the best way to convince this man to take a chance on me. I cleared my throat as I peeled a lock of icy hair from my cheek. "Sorry, I'm a bit tetchy. I barely slept."

"Neither did I." West crouched, his arms locked around his knees, and I sat in the snow, not caring about the dampness that seeped through my pants. Lady Lola bounded up, nuzzling her head under my arm, and I took the opportunity to pet her while I steadied my nerves.

"West, I'm so sorry about last night. I let my insecurities get the better of me. Here you were, holding out this sparkling dream of a future on this fancy platter, and it, well, it overwhelmed me. What if I couldn't live up to what you wanted? What if I couldn't be the girlfriend of a man who dates rock stars and lives in sunny California and holds the door for Harry Styles at Whole Foods? I'm just me, West. I live a pretty mundane life, in a small town in Scotland. I got scared."

"Yeah, I gathered that. And, boring?" West held his hands out in the air. "What, particularly, is boring about here? Was it the unicorn? Or the standing stones that grant wishes? Or the ghost coo and broonie who rescued us from a snowstorm? Or perhaps those pesky Kelpies really drag the whole town down with their boring appearances? Yes, Maisie. What a drag it is here. I can't believe I didn't cut my time short."

Damn it, but the man had a point. I sniffed.

"Noted," I said, wiping more snow from my face.

"Maisie—"

"Truly I was just overwhelmed, and I took the easy route of pushing you away. I should've talked to you about this. About all of this." I waved my hand in the air. "Instead, I was so scared of you telling me you were going to leave that I kept putting off the conversation. When the manuscript—"

"Listen, Maisie. That is something I should apologize for." West stopped me when I tried to speak. "I should have asked you first. The book is your special project, and I took liberties with it that I shouldn't have. I was just so excited about the story and hoped to be able to help you, is all. It came from a good place, even if I executed it poorly."

"Thank you," I said, blinking back the tears that threatened. Seriously, was I ever going to stop crying? "I appreciate that, and I should have accepted the gift for what it was—a well-intentioned attempt to help."

"I'll do better next time."

Next time. Now the tears did spill over. This wonderful man wasn't giving up on me. Wiping the tears with the back of my frozen hands I looked at him with my heart in my eyes.

"I love the way you see me, West. I wanted to *be* the

woman that *you* see, the writer that you admire, the strong Scottish lass who fears nothing. And last night, when you told me about the manuscript and that you were leaving, I panicked. In that moment, I couldn't be the woman that you thought you knew. After I calmed down, and Agnes kicked my arse some, I realized, I can be. No, I *am* that woman. I believe in *us*. I believe in myself. I believe in our future together. Whatever it may hold. And I choose you, West, to build a future together with. That's my Christmas gift to you, West."

"But you already got me a gift."

West's lips quirked when I glared daggers at him. I'd just poured my heart out and here he was making jokes?

"I guess I'll have to get you another gift then, to make it even." Reaching forward, West put his hands under my arms and hauled me to standing in one smooth motion. "How about a plane ticket to California?"

"Seriously?" I asked, wiping tears as my teeth started to chatter from the cold and my nerves.

"Seriously. Come stay for a bit. If you can leave work, of course. You can meet your new agent, John. We'll walk on the beach. Talk about life. Figure things out. Not everything has to be decided in a day, you know." West brushed a tear away with his finger and my heart fluttered in my chest.

"You're not giving up on me?"

"As long as we keep choosing each other, I'm all in, Maisie."

"Och, thank you." I jumped up, wrapping my arms around his neck, claiming his mouth in an icy kiss, my body shivering against his. I wanted to hold on to him and never let go. West angled his head, deepening the kiss, and my core began to heat, needing him close to me.

When a snowball exploded against both of our heads, we dove apart, shrieking.

Clyde bellowed behind us, dancing on his hooves, the Christmas lights in his horns blinking wildly. Delighted with himself, he dug his head in the snow and flipped some more onto his nose, arming himself. Brice popped up next to him, his eyes glinting beneath his tiny red hat, a snowball in hand. West grabbed my arm.

"Run!"

EPILOGUE

Maisie

Hogmanay.

It was a time of endings and new beginnings, as we said goodbye to the year before and welcomed in the new. Nobody did New Year's quite like the Scots, and I'd always enjoyed the celebrations surrounding the day. I'd even gone to Edinburgh a time or two, to join in the celebrations that lasted into the wee hours of the morning, with flaming torches and parades and fireworks. There was nothing quite like it.

But now, quite simply, I missed West.

He'd kept his flight on Christmas Day, and as much as I hadn't wanted him to go home, I also knew his mother had needed him. We'd kept in contact, talking several times a day, but the future felt ... undecided. West repeatedly assured me that he'd sort things out once his mother was on her feet again, and I took him at his word.

Turns out, patience was not my strong suit.

Sighing, I stirred my drink with my straw.

"What's got you so mopey?" Shona, a local gardener, flower designer, and all-over green thumb type, nudged me.

"Just missing West. It was so fast and furious and then he was gone. Two weeks and the man just up and changed my life." I snapped my fingers. I'd met Shona for lunch a few days prior and had filled her in.

"Plus he's gone for midnight." Shona sighed and dropped her face into her fist. A pretty blonde with sparkling blue eyes, I was surprised someone hadn't snapped her up. She was a lovely woman. "That's one thing I'm not too keen on. Not having a strapping lad for a kiss when the ball drops."

"Did someone call for a strapping lad?" As if on cue, Graham leaned over the bar and winked at us.

"Try it and West will have your head." I shook my head at Graham.

"Like an American can take me," Graham scoffed, offended.

"And if he doesn't, I will." Agnes joined us.

"You don't even know what we were talking about," Graham protested, the light of war coming into his eyes.

"Surely I don't need to be a lipreader to know you were hitting on these two lovely lasses, do I then?" Agnes arched a brow.

"And why shouldn't I be then? Beautiful women such as these need to be complimented. Worshipped. Adored."

"Did someone say adored?" Esther sidled up, wearing a Christmas jumper that read *Moo-y Christmas* and had a picture of a Highland coo with a Santa hat on it. "I'm accepting all adoration from handsome men."

"As you well should be." Graham snatched her hand and kissed it dramatically. Esther shot him a cheeky look.

"Och, lad. The things that I could *teach* you."

I choked on the sip of drink that I'd taken and for the first time ever, I saw Graham's cheeks pinken. Agnes howled in delight.

"Good on ya, Esther. Give the lad a run for his money."

Esther fluttered her lashes before turning to us. "Did you hear the latest gossip?"

"We do love gossip, so tell, tell," Shona insisted, giving Graham an excuse to retreat.

"See for yourself." Esther nodded to a small table by the fireplace.

My jaw dropped.

"Is that Meredith and Fergus?" I asked, delighted.

"It is." Esther beamed. "Apparently, he was quite taken with her gingerbread decorating style, and they stayed after to discuss techniques, and well, one thing led to another, and soon they were on to other techniques if you catch my drift."

"We do, we do," I said hastily, wincing at the imagery that threatened.

"Go Meredith?" Agnes said, in a question.

"It's a good thing. Apparently, he has strong hands. From shearing all those sheep."

"Oh God," Agnes whispered at my side. "A fact I did not need to know."

"It's almost time," Graham shouted, quieting the music and turning the radio up to the countdown. Together, the busy pub shouted down the final seconds of the year. At the stroke of midnight, the pub exploded in celebration and Shona caught me in a hug.

Graham leaned over the bar, snagged Agnes's chin in his hand, and gave her a searing kiss that had my toes curling in my shoes just looking at it.

"Prickly woman," Graham said, as he pulled away.

"Cheeky bastard," Agnes grumbled.

"Happiest of New Year's to you, darling." Graham winked and returned to filling pints and Agnes turned to find us all staring with our arms crossed over our chests. "What?"

"What was *that*?" I asked, circling my finger in the air.

"*That* was nothing."

"It didn't look like nothing." Esther clucked her tongue. "He's got good hands too."

Agnes rolled her eyes, looking away toward the door. "Look—a first footing!"

The pub quieted at her words to see who would be the first one through the door. It was an old tradition in Scotland, where the first person through the door would bring gifts of well-wishes for the new year, like a coin for wealth, coal for heat, and so on.

When West walked in, carrying a bag of goodies, my eyes filled. Jumping up, I ran to him, not caring that the pub watched me, and threw my arms around his neck. Droplets of water from the snow outside clung to his glasses, and his cheeks were red from the cold. He caught me with one arm, pulling me tight, and bent his head for a kiss that reminded me just how single-minded the man could be when he was focused.

And yes, my toes curled in my shoes.

When I came up for air, the pub was cheering, and tears were running down my face.

"What are you *doing* here? I didn't think you could make it back so soon," I gasped, happiness making me feel giddy and jumpy as I pulled him over to the bar.

"I didn't either. But I sorted it out, as you would say."

"Hey, mate. Great to have you back. Anything you hear about me hitting on Maisie is a straight lie, by the way." Graham clasped West's hand. He narrowed his eyes at the bartender.

"Coward," Agnes said cheerfully.

"You making time with my girl?"

My girl. The words made me giddy. Well, West being near made me a wee bit giddy. The night shifted from melancholy to happy, the pub taking on a warm glow of cheer.

"I make time with all the girls, West."

"Truer words have never been spoken." Agnes glowered into her pint of cider.

"I brought gifts." West intervened and nudged the bag at Graham who gleefully pulled out gifts for everyone to see.

"Let's see if the American can do it right. A dollar?" Graham shook his head sadly as he held up the dollar bill. "At this exchange rate, lad? I should be offended."

"In fairness, it didn't say how much money to give," West protested.

"Sea salt?" Graham held up a bottle of salt with palm trees on the label.

"From California. Listen … again, it just said salt."

"I'll accept it." Next, Graham held up a tin. "Let's see. Shortbread?"

"My mom made it. She's a champion baker, but nervous that the Scots won't accept it. Be nice, or I'll make you be nice."

Did I like this domineering side of West? Maybe just a bit too much. I grinned, snuggling closer as Graham took a dutiful bite.

"Perfection. She could be Scottish herself."

The pub cheered. Esther eyed the tin.

"I'd better judge for myself on that." Esther took a piece, and I waited, praying she wouldn't insult West's mother. I'd only met the woman via video call, but she seemed lovely.

"That'll do just fine. You can tell your mother she has a knack for it."

"Now the real test ... a ..." Graham scowled at the airport travel-sized bottle of Jack Daniels he pulled from the bag.

"You didn't," I gasped.

The tone of the pub changed, and Esther whistled low. Fierce murmurings ran through the crowd. Fergus stood.

"I'd run if I was you, lad."

"Oof, you Scots are a touchy bunch, aren't you?" West dug into his coat and pulled out a bottle of Balvenie with a bow wrapped around it. Graham audibly exhaled.

"I was about to kick you out, lad, and that's no joke."

"I know it." West grinned and the tension eased in the room. Graham turned, flipping the dial on the music, and returned with a dram for West. Still he stood, his arms wrapped around me, and I leaned into him, looking up shyly. I still couldn't believe he was here.

"You're here." I grinned when he flicked a finger down

my cheek, a habit I loved of his. "Don't you have to go back to classes?"

"Nope." West grinned when my mouth dropped open.

"You quit?" Hope bloomed.

"Mmm, not yet. But I might. I have an interview. In Glasgow."

"No way," I breathed. "Does that mean—"

"It means nothing at the moment. I took a sabbatical from my job, which, by the way, they were none too pleased about, so I may very well be quitting or be asked to leave. But I had a long talk with your new agent, John, when I got home."

I'd signed with John Batemen after West had walked me through the contract, and already I'd started outlining the next book. I'd been so busy focusing on the rejections coming through that I'd quite forgotten that I could just crack on with writing a new book. I found my excitement for writing again, and even if my first novel didn't kick off, I was just happy to be back creating stories. It was the first step toward a dream I was building for myself, and I had West to thank for nudging me out of my holding pattern. I'd been right about this man. He did have the power to change the trajectory of my future. *For the better.*

"Turns out, I have a few book ideas in me as well. Being here ..."—West leaned in and lowered his voice—"around all these incredible myths coming to life? Well, it led me down a path of sketching out some great story ideas. Fiction, naturally, but man, oh man, I think it would be fun to write. John seemed to agree. He's signed me as well."

"Shut up." I slapped his chest, a grin spreading on my face. "We're going to write books together?"

"Well, maybe not co-authored. But next to each other if you don't mind me basking in your literary greatness."

A laugh bubbled up as I imagined West bent, furiously typing, a concentrated look on his face. The only problem I could see was ...

"Och, I do love that look you get when you're focused on something. I might be a bit of a distraction for you." I trailed my finger down his chest, flirting with him.

"Something that I wholeheartedly look forward to." West caught my hand before it reached his waistband and pressed a kiss into my palm. Turning, he caught Esther staring at us, her eyebrows raised.

"What's that look for, Esther?" West asked.

"Nothing." Esther grinned. "I just noticed what nice hands you have, West. Nice hands, indeed."

Looking for added sparkle and fun this Christmas? Be sure to order one of these limited edition Christmas Coo designs! I will be wearing the All I want for Christmas is Moo design when I visit family in Scotland this December. Keep an eye out for pictures in my newsletter and on social media. Sparkle on!

Shop today at triciaomalley.myshopify.com

A KILT FOR CHRISTMAS

Christmas Coo Collection

www.triciaomalley.com

AFTERWORD

Author's note

I had not planned to write this book. Nope, not in the slightest. I was already over my max for the year when it came to writing, and I'd promised myself some downtime to recharge. Apparently, my characters had other ideas, and they can be quite annoying when they want to be. Clyde insisted on decorating himself for Christmas, my readers kept asking to return to Loren Brae, and even the infamous Book Bitches from *Starting Over Scottish* pestered me for a story. And I was only too happy to bow to everyone's demands. The truth is, I find it hard to take time off unless I am traveling. I *love* writing. I mean, let's be honest here – I get to make up stories for a living. How cool is that? It certainly wasn't a hardship to return to Loren Brae and have this much fun with a Christmas story. Thank you, darling readers, for always supporting me wherever I may take you. Sometimes it is a bit of a wild ride – ghost coos, unicorns, and broonies – oh my! Nevertheless, you all

AFTERWORD

embrace it with endless enthusiasm, and I couldn't be more grateful to have you along for the ride.

Sending all sorts of sparkles your way to light up this time of year, when the days grow shorter and the weather turns colder. This is when the world needs your sparkles the most, so never forget to keep on shining.

Sparkle on, friends!

Tricia O'Malley

WILD SCOTTISH ROSE

Sneak Peak – Wild Scottish Rose

Shona

"I *said* I wanted Calla lilies."

I tensed as the bride's voice cut through the din of chatter where my team, as well as the venue staff, were setting up the reception area for the wedding that evening. Turning, I pasted a polite smile on my face as the bride, Kennedy Williams of Dallas, Texas, bore down on me. Her pretty face was screwed up in anger and her eyes were alight with battle.

Life was going to be difficult for Kennedy if she got this angry over flowers.

"I'm certain that you didn't. But I'll just double-check the order form if you'd like confirmation?" I pulled up my phone and flipped through the orders which I had neatly organized in a file, even though I was well aware that *Miss* Kennedy Williams had ordered white roses for her centerpieces. The arrangements were simple and beautiful, as instructed on the order form, and I'd chosen roses at varying stages of bloom to add depth to the centerpieces. Even though white roses were the most common order I received from brides, I still enjoyed working with the flower. It was one of my favorites, after all. Even more exciting? An opportunity to decorate at Òran Mór, a fabulous reception venue in Glasgow housed in a renovated church. It was my first time traveling this far for a wedding, and I was hoping to enjoy a bit of the city after we finished setting up.

Life in Loren Brae was lovely, and while I enjoyed the pace, it was still nice to get to the city on occasion for some excitement. And *shopping*. My heart did a little dance thinking about how I'd carefully saved up to buy some extravagant lingerie. It was a secret passion of mine, because much of my life was spent mucking in the dirt, and it was useless to buy pretty clothes that would just get ruined. Now, my earlier excitement at working with the incredible team at Òran Mór, and the prospect of a shopping trip, dimmed. Already I could see my chance to shop being pulled away from me as I mentally readied myself to change all the arrangements right before the reception. It would be a mad dash, and I'd have to call in some favors from local florists, but it could be done if needed.

"White roses?" Kennedy sneered as I pulled up her order. "How positively boring. I definitely ordered the lilies."

"No," I began, turning my phone to show her the screen.

"Lilies? Aren't lilies for funerals?" A voice interrupted us, and a shiver danced across the back of my neck.

"What?" A look of confusion crossed Kennedy's face and she whirled on the man who approached us.

I suppose approach was a casual word for how this man strode confidently through the hall, outfitted in a perfectly fit tuxedo, with a tartan bow and matching pocket square. He moved like a panther, his eyes darting across the room, and seeming to take in every detail at once. When they landed on me, his assessment stopped, and a smile landed on his lips. Close-cropped dark hair, lively blue eyes, and broad shoulders completed the package and I found myself desperately wishing I'd dressed up.

Which was silly, really, considering that dressing up didn't make sense with the amount of manual labor it took to decorate an entire reception hall with flowers. It wasn't just putting vases of flowers on the tables – there were garlands to be hung, vines to be entwined, and lighting to be added. Frankly, I wasn't even sure I owned anything that this type of man would find appealing. Either way, jeans, a t-shirt, and trainers were the smart choice for my line of work. And that was me. Sensible to my core.

What was it about this man that instantly made me *not* want to be sensible?

"Lilies are traditionally used for funerals. You wouldn't want people to think that your marriage is a death, would you?" The man turned to Kennedy, who looked up at him with annoyance on her face.

"Damn it, Owen. Why do you always come in and screw things up when I'm just trying to get things handled?" Kennedy demanded.

"Kennedy, if I may? It does say here on your form that you ordered the roses. See?" I brandished my phone, hoping to head off an argument between these two, but neither bothered to glance my way.

"See? The pretty flower lady says you ordered roses. Frankly, I'm surprised at that choice as well," Owen said. He crossed his arms over his chest and gave Kennedy a wry smile.

"What's wrong with roses?" Kennedy demanded, immediately jumping ship from the lily train to roses. Relief passed through me. If she was going to defend roses, then maybe I'd be off the hook and could get back to decorating. Easing back a step, hoping to leave them to their argument, I caught the eye of my assistant who hovered nearby with a vase in hand and a questioning look on her face. I gave her a subtle nod, and she continued to set up while I waited to hear the outcome of this discussion.

"Nothing, of course, as these vases are perfection in their own right." Owen slid me a grin and I'm pretty sure my insides melted. His American accent held a hint of the south and somewhere else, but I wasn't well-versed enough in accents to place it. I found myself wanting to inch closer, to be drawn into his hemisphere, just to listen to him talk.

Never had I met a man with so much charisma before.

Apparently, I wasn't the only one who felt this way, as I caught more than one of the event staff giving him appreciative looks.

"It's just that..." Owen continued, tapping a finger against his lips. "We're in Scotland, right? I'm surprised you didn't go with something more traditional to the venue."

My stomach dropped. If I had to run out and find thistles, I would, even if it meant cutting them from the side of the road.

"You're right," Kennedy gasped and gripped his arm. "What was I thinking? What should I add in?"

"Haggis, naturally."

My heart skipped a beat, and I pressed my lips together to hold back a burst of laughter. Surely the bride had to know that haggis was a dish, not a flower. My eyes widened as Kennedy whirled on me.

"*You*. I need you to get wild haggis for the centerpieces." Kennedy snapped her fingers at me, her eyes bright with determination, and I blinked at her as I tried to come up with an excuse that wouldn't embarrass the bride. She didn't seem like the type to be able to laugh at a joke at her own expense.

"Well..." I began and Owen cut me off.

"In fact, you'll probably want haggis added to the bridal bouquet as well. Oh, and the boutonnieres for the men. Maybe the bartenders could make a haggis drink?"

"Of course! Like my lavender-infused martinis that I love." Kennedy turned and stormed across the room to the bar, and I was grateful for the momentary reprieve, though now I had to come up with a way to tell her that I wasn't about to put meat flowers in her bouquet.

"I'm probably going to hell. But I do so love winding her up. I'm Owen, by the way." Owen held out his hand and I took it automatically, though my stomach twisted in knots about how to deal with this latest catastrophe.

"Shona," I said, faintly, my eyes on where Kennedy berated one of the bartenders about a haggis martini.

"My apologies, Shona, that you have to deal with Kennedy. She's not always this difficult..." Owen trailed off as he squinted his eyes. "Actually, nevermind, she is. In fact, I'm now warming to the idea of haggis in her flowers."

"But…I can't…possibly…" I held my hands up, at a loss for words.

"I think you can do anything you put your mind to." Owen pursed his lips and studied me, clearly used to people falling in line with his plans. I wanted to, I *really* wanted to, because there was something about the wicked glint in his eyes that made me want to be naughty even just for a bit.

I was *so* done with weddings.

It wasn't that all of them were awful, or anything like that, I was just over doing flowers for weddings. The stress never lived up to the enjoyment for me. I'd much rather be back home, nurturing my plants, and selling my wares at farmers markets. It was my comfort zone and this…well, *this* was not what I needed right now.

"Shona!" Kennedy shouted from across the room, stomping her foot, and Owen intervened.

"I'll handle her. Just get your decorations out as you see fit. She'll be happy enough once she's married." It came out as an order, and I found my attraction to this man instantly diminishing. Men like him? Yeah, they were used to dealing with women like Kennedy. He could very well handle it while I stuck to what I knew best – plants.

"Yes, sir. Whatever you say sir." I infused enough syrupy sweetness in my voice, so Owen knew that I was annoyed with him and walked away.

"Sassy. I like it." Owen winked at me. Damn it, but I found the wink sexy, and I hated myself for doing so. It was so cliché. The wink. The charm. The casual ease in a tuxedo. Owen was not my type of people. Why I even found myself attracted to him was beyond me.

"Your opinion matters little to me," I surprised myself by saying, and the grin widened on Owen's face before he sauntered away. What was wrong with me? I'd just insulted a client's guest. That would *not* bode well for my business. Even if I'd promised myself that I was done with weddings, I still didn't want to get any bad online reviews.

"Why is the bride screaming about haggis?" my assistant whispered in my ear. I kept my eyes trained on Owen as he pulled Kennedy away from the bar.

"Who is that?" I asked, turning to unwrap the padding from around a vase.

"The one who knows exactly what he's about?" My assistant fanned her face, and I rolled my eyes. "That's the brother."

Of course it was. Nothing like directly insulting a family member. I'd have to apologize later. But for now, I needed to make a plan.

"Do we still have the extra bucket of white heather in the van?" The bride hadn't asked for it, but I typically brought some along in case any spots needed filling.

"We do. Are we adding it?"

"We are. If anyone asks…it's wild haggis."

Fall in love with the much-anticipated fourth book in the
Enchanted Highlands series.
Order Wild Scottish Rose today!

ALSO BY TRICIA O'MALLEY

THE ISLE OF DESTINY SERIES

Stone Song

Sword Song

Spear Song

Sphere Song

A completed series in Kindle Unlimited.

Available in audio, e-book & paperback!

"Love this series. I will read this multiple times. Keeps you on the edge of your seat. It has action, excitement and romance all in one series."

- Amazon Review

THE ENCHANTED HIGHLANDS

Wild Scottish Knight
Wild Scottish Love
A Kilt for Christmas
Wild Scottish Rose

"I love everything Tricia O'Malley has ever written and "Wild Scottish Knight" is no exception. The new setting for this magical journey is Scotland, the home of her new husband and soulmate. Tricia's love for her husbands country shows in every word she writes. I have always wanted to visit Scotland but have never had the time and money. Having read "Wild Scottish Knight" I feel I have begun to to experience Scotland in a way few see it. I am ready to go see Loren Brae, the castle and all its magical creatures, for myself. Tricia O'Malley makes the fantasy world of Loren Brae seem real enough to touch!"

-Amazon Review

Available in audio, e-book, hardback, paperback and is included in your Kindle Unlimited subscription.

THE WILDSONG SERIES

Song of the Fae

Melody of Flame

Chorus of Ashes

Lyric of Wind

"The magic of Fae is so believable. I read these books in one sitting and can't wait for the next one. These are books you will reread many times."

- Amazon Review

A completed series in Kindle Unlimited.

Available in audio, e-book & paperback!

THE SIREN ISLAND SERIES

Good Girl

Up to No Good

A Good Chance

Good Moon Rising

Too Good to Be True

A Good Soul

In Good Time

A completed series in Kindle Unlimited.
Available in audio, e-book & paperback!

"Love her books and was excited for a totally new and different one! Once again, she did NOT disappoint! Magical in multiple ways and on multiple levels. Her writing style, while similar to that of Nora Roberts, kicks it up a notch!! I want to visit that island, stay in the B&B and meet the gals who run it! The characters are THAT real!!!" - Amazon Review

THE ALTHEA ROSE SERIES

One Tequila

Tequila for Two

Tequila Will Kill Ya (Novella)

Three Tequilas

Tequila Shots & Valentine Knots (Novella)

Tequila Four

A Fifth of Tequila

A Sixer of Tequila

Seven Deadly Tequilas

Eight Ways to Tequila

Tequila for Christmas (Novella)

"Not my usual genre but couldn't resist the Florida Keys setting. I was hooked from the first page. A fun read with just the right amount of crazy! Will definitely follow this series."- Amazon Review

A completed series in Kindle Unlimited.

Available in audio, e-book & paperback!

THE MYSTIC COVE SERIES

Wild Irish Heart

Wild Irish Eyes

Wild Irish Soul

Wild Irish Rebel

Wild Irish Roots: Margaret & Sean

Wild Irish Witch

Wild Irish Grace

Wild Irish Dreamer

Wild Irish Christmas (Novella)

Wild Irish Sage

Wild Irish Renegade

Wild Irish Moon

"I have read thousands of books and a fair percentage have been romances. Until I read Wild Irish Heart, I never had a book actually make me believe in love."- Amazon Review

A completed series in Kindle Unlimited.
Available in audio, e-book & paperback!

STAND ALONE NOVELS

Ms. Bitch

"Ms. Bitch is sunshine in a book! An uplifting story of fighting your way through heartbreak and making your own version of happily-ever-after."

~Ann Charles, USA Today Bestselling Author

Starting Over Scottish

Grumpy. Meet Sunshine.

She's American. He's Scottish. She's looking for a fresh start. He's returning to rediscover his roots.

One Way Ticket

A funny and captivating beach read where booking a one-way ticket to paradise means starting over, letting go, and taking a chance on love…one more time

10 out of 10 - The BookLife Prize

ACKNOWLEDGMENTS

Thank you, as always, to my incredible readers for continuing on this lovely journey with me. I know I say it all the time, but I really do have the best readers. While I love nothing more than to put stories about love and light into the world, I can't help but feel so lucky to have that love mirrored back to me from all of you. Thank you, from the bottom of my heart, for your support. Even when I can't respond to every email or social media comment, please know that I feel your support.

Thank you to Marion, my fabulous editor, who constantly makes me laugh with her pointed feedback and entertaining comments.

Thank you to the Scotsman's family for their help with this story, from answering random questions about all things Scottish to proofing and editing the final product. You all do such a fabulous job in helping to make my books shine.

Finally, thank you to my handsome Scotsman, a man I'm lucky enough to call my partner, my best friend, and my soul mate. Love you forever.

CONTACT ME

I hope my books have added a little magick into your life. If you have a moment to add some to my day, you can help by telling your friends and leaving a review. Word-of-mouth is the most powerful way to share my stories. Thank you.

Love books? What about fun giveaways? Nope? Okay, can I entice you with underwater photos and cute dogs? Let's stay friends! Sign up for my newsletter and contact me at my website.

www.triciaomalley.com

Or find me on Facebook and Instagram.
@triciaomalleyauthor

Printed in Great Britain
by Amazon